"I hope you'll let Davy and ~~me show our appreciation by~~ buying you breakfast, Dr. St. Sebastian."

"Thanks, but I've already had breakfast."

No way Mike was letting this gorgeous creature get away. "Dinner, then."

"I'm, uh, I'm here with my family."

"I am, too. Unfortunately." He made a face at his nephew, who giggled and returned the exaggerated grimace. "I'd be even more grateful if you give me an excuse to get away from them for a while."

"Well..."

He didn't miss her brief hesitation. Or her quick glance at *his* left hand. The white imprint of his wedding ring had long since faded. Too bad he couldn't say the same for the inner scars. Shoving the disaster of his marriage into the dark hole where it belonged, Mike overrode her apparent doubts.

"Where are you staying?"

She took her time replying. Those exotic eyes looked him up and down.

"We're at the Camino del Ray," she said finally, almost reluctantly. "It's about a half mile up the beach."

Mike suppressed a smile. "I know where it is. I'll pick you up at seven-thirty."

* * *

The Texan's Royal M.D. is part of the
Duchess Diaries series—
Two royal granddaughters on their way
to happily ever after!

* * *

If you're on Twitter,
tell us what you think of Harlequin Desire!
#harlequindesire

Dear Reader,

As a history buff, I've read extensively about the Austrian-Hungarian Empire. Also about one of the empire's most tragic figures—Elisabeth Amalie Eugenie, Empress of Austria and Queen of Hungary. Sisi, as she was known, lost her only son in a murder-suicide pact. She herself was assassinated by an anarchist in Geneva, Switzerland, in 1898.

Recently, my husband and I seemed to be tracing Sisi's footsteps in our travels. We visited the Hapsburg Palaces in Vienna and Budapest, her retreat in Corfu, and many hunting lodges and grand hotels where she stayed. And the more I learned about this incredibly beautiful and tragic woman, the more I wanted to craft a modern-day character along her royal lines.

Thus the Duchess Diaries—and Charlotte, the Grand Duchess of Karlenburgh—were born. I hope you've enjoyed her and all the St. Sebastians as much as I have!

Merline

THE TEXAN'S ROYAL M.D.

MERLINE LOVELACE

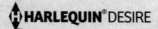

ISBN-13: 978-0-373-73370-5

The Texan's Royal M.D.

Copyright © 2015 by Merline Lovelace

Printed in U.S.A.

www.Harlequin.com

A career Air Force officer, **Merline Lovelace** served at bases all over the world. When she hung up her uniform for the last time she decided to combine her love of adventure with a flair for storytelling, basing many of her tales on her own experiences in uniform. Since then she's produced more than ninety action-packed sizzlers, many of which have made the *USA TODAY* and Waldenbooks bestseller lists. Over eleven million copies of her books are available in some thirty countries.

When she's not tied to her keyboard, Merline enjoys reading, chasing little white balls around the fairways of Oklahoma and traveling to new and exotic locales with her handsome husband, Al. Check her website, merlinelovelace.com, or friend her on Facebook for news and information about her latest releases.

Books by Merline Lovelace

Harlequin Desire

The Paternity Promise
The Paternity Proposition

The Duchess Diaries Series
A Business Engagement
The Diplomat's Pregnant Bride
Her Unforgettable Royal Lover
The Texan's Royal M.D.

Visit the Author Profile page
at Harlequin.com for more titles.

Prologue

I seem to have come full circle. For so many years my life centered on my darling granddaughters. Now they're grown and are busy with lives of their own. Quiet, elegant Sarah has an adoring husband, a blossoming career as an author and her first child on the way. And Eugenia, my carefree, high-spirited Eugenia, is the wife of a United Nations diplomat and the mother of twins. She fills both roles so joyously, so effortlessly.

I do wish I could say the same of Dominic, my impossibly handsome great-nephew. Dom still hasn't adjusted to the fact that he now carries the title of Grand Duke of Karlenburgh. I've caught him rolling his shoulders as though he itches for his previous life as an undercover agent. Then his glance strays to his wife and his restlessness fades instantly. Natalie's so demure, so sweet and so startlingly intelligent!

She quite astonishes us all with the depth of her knowledge of the most arcane subjects—including the history of my beloved Karlenburgh.

These days I live vicariously through Dom's sister, Anastazia. I'll admit I played shamelessly on our distant kinship to convince

Zia to reside with me during her pediatric residency in New York City. She's only a few short months away from finishing the grueling three-year program. She should be feeling nothing but elation that the end is in sight. Yet I sense that something's troubling her. Something she doesn't wish to talk about, even with me. I shan't force the issue. I don't condone unwelcome intrusiveness, even by the most concerned and well-meaning. I do hope, however, that the vacation I've engineered for the family over the coming holidays eases some of the worry Zia hides behind her so bright, so lovely smile.

From the diary of Charlotte,
Grand Duchess of Karlenburgh

One

Zia almost didn't hear the shout over the roar of the waves. Preoccupied with the decision hanging over her like an executioner's ax, she'd slipped away for an early-morning jog along the glistening silver shoreline of Galveston Island, Texas. Although the Gulf of Mexico offered a glorious symphony of green water and lacy surf, Zia barely noticed the ever-changing seascape. She needed time and the endless, empty shore to think. Solitude to wrestle with her private demons.

She loved her family—her adored older brother, Dominic; her great-aunt Charlotte, who'd practically adopted her; the cousins she'd grown so close to in the past few years; their spouses and lively offspring. But spending the Christmas holidays in Galveston with the entire St. Sebastian clan hadn't allowed much time for soul-searching. Zia only had three more days to decide. Three days before she returned to New York and...

"Go get it, Buster!"

Sunk in thought, she might have blocked out the gleeful shout if she hadn't spent the past two and a half years as a pediatric resident at Kravis Children's Hospital, part of the Mount Sinai hospital network in New York City. All those rewarding, gut-wrenching hours working with infants and young kids had fine-tuned Zia's instincts to the point that her mind tagged the voice instantly as belonging to a five- or six-year-old male with a healthy set of lungs.

A smile formed as she angled toward the sound. Her sneakers slapping the hard-packed sand at the water's edge, she jogged backward a few paces and watched the child who raced through the shallows about thirty yards behind her. Red haired and freckle faced, he was in hot pursuit of a stubby brown-and-white terrier. The dog, in turn, chased a soaring Frisbee. Boy and pet plunged joyously through the shallow surf, oblivious to everything but the purple plastic disc.

Zia's smile widened at their antics but took a quick downward turn when she scanned the shore behind them and failed to spot an adult. Where were the boy's parents? Or his nanny, given that this stretch of beach included several glitzy, high-dollar resorts? Or even an older sibling? The boy was too young to be cavorting in the surf unsupervised.

Anger sliced into her, swift and icy hot. She'd had to deal with the results of parental negligence far too often to view it with complacency. She was feeling the heat of that anger, the sick disgust she had to swallow while treating abused or neglected children, when another cry wrenched her attention back to the boy. This one was high and reedy and tinged with panic.

Her heart stuttering, Zia saw he'd lunged into waves to meet the terrier paddling toward shore with the Frisbee clenched between his jaws. She knew the bank dropped off steeply at that point. Too steeply! And the undertow when the tide went out was strong enough to drag down full-grown adult.

She was already racing back to the boy when he disappeared. She locked her frantic gaze on the spot where his red hair sank below the waves, crashed into the water and made a flying dive.

She couldn't see him! The receding tide had churned up too much sand. Grit stung her eyes. The ocean hissed and boiled in her ears. She flung out her arms, thrashed them blindly. Her lungs on fire, she thrust out of the water like a dolphin spooked by a killer whale and arced back in.

Just before she went under she caught a glimpse of the terrier's rear end pointed at the sky. The dog dove down at the same instant Zia did and led her to the child being dragged along by the undertow. She shot past the dog. Grabbed the boy's wrist. Propelled upward with fast, hard scissor kicks. She had to swim parallel to the shore for several desperate moments before the vicious current loosened its grip enough for her to cut toward dry land.

He wasn't breathing when she turned him on his back and started CPR. Her head told her he hadn't been in the water long enough to suffer severe oxygen deprivation, but his lips were tinged with blue. Completely focused, Zia ignored the dog that whined and pawed frantic trenches in the sand by the boy's head. Ignored as well the thud of running feet, the offers of help, the deep shout that was half panic, half prayer.

"Davy! Jesus!"

The small chest twitched under Zia's palms. A moment later, the boy's back arched and seawater spewed from his mouth. With a silent prayer of thanksgiving to Saint Stephen, patron saint of her native Hungary, Zia rolled him onto his side and held his head while he hacked up most of what he'd swallowed. When he was done, she eased him down again. His nose ran in twin streams and tears spurted from his eyes but, amazingly, he gulped back his sobs.

"Wh...? What happened?"

She gave him a reassuring smile. "You went out too far and got dragged in by the undertow."

"Did I...? Did I get drowned?"

"Almost."

He hooked an arm around his anxious pet's neck while a slowly dawning excitement edged out the confusion and fear in his brown eyes. "Wait till I tell Mommy and Kevin and *abuelita* and..." His gaze shifted right and latched on to something just over Zia's shoulder. "Uncle Mickey! Uncle Mickey! Did you hear that? I almost got drowned!"

"Yeah, brat, I heard."

It was the same deep baritone that had barely registered with Zia a moment ago. The panic was gone, though, replaced by relief colored with what sounded like reluctant amusement.

Jézus, Mária és József! Didn't this idiot appreciate how close a call his nephew had just had? Incensed, Zia shoved to her feet and spun toward him. She was just about to let loose with both barrels when she realized his amused drawl had been show for the boy's sake. Despite the seemingly laconic reply, his hands were balled into fists and his faded University of Texas T-shirt stretched across taut shoulders.

Very wide shoulders, she couldn't help but note, topped by a tree trunk of a neck and a square chin showing just a hint of a dimple. With her trained clinician's eye for detail, Zia also noted that his nose looked as though it had gotten crosswise of a fist sometime in his past and his eyes gleamed as deep a green as the ocean. His hair was a rich, dark sorrel and cut rigorously short.

The rest of him wasn't bad, either. She formed a fleeting impression of a broad chest, muscular thighs emerging from ragged cutoffs, and bare feet sporting worn leather flip-flops. Then those sea-green eyes flashed her a grateful look and he went down on one knee beside his nephew.

"You, young man," he said as he helped the boy sit up,

"are in deep doo-doo. You know darn well you're not allowed to come down to the beach alone."

"Buster needed to go out."

"I repeat, you are *not* allowed to come down to beach alone."

Zia shrugged off the remnants of the rage that had hit her when she'd thought the boy was allowed to roam unsupervised. She also had to hide a smile at the pitiful note that crept into Davy's voice. Like all five- or six-year olds, he had the whine down pat.

"You said Buster was my 'sponsibility when you gave him to me, Uncle Mickey. You said I had to walk him 'n feed him 'n pick up his poop 'n…"

"We'll continue this discussion later."

Whoa! Even Zia blinked at the *that's enough* finality in the uncle's voice.

"How do you feel?" he asked the boy.

"'Kay."

"Good enough to stand up?"

"Sure."

With the youthful resilience that never failed to amaze Zia, the kid flashed a cheeky grin and scrambled to his feet. His pet woofed encouragement, and both boy and dog would have scampered off if the uncle hadn't laid a restraining hand on his nephew's shoulder.

"Don't you have something you want to say to this lady?"

"Thanks for not letting me get drowned."

"You're welcome."

His uncle kept him in place by a firm grip on his wet T-shirt and held out his other hand to Zia. "I'm Mike Brennan. I can't thank you enough for what you did for Davy."

She took the offered hand, registered its strength and warmth as it folded around hers. "Anastazia St. Sebastian. I'm glad I got to him in time."

* * *

The sheer terror that had rocked Mike's world when he'd spotted this woman hauling Davy's limp body out of the sea had receded enough now for him to focus on her for the first time. Closer inspection damn near rocked him back on his flip-flops again.

Her wet, glistening black hair hung to just below her shoulders. Her eyes were almost as dark as her hair and had just the suggestion of a slant to them. And any supermodel on the planet would have killed for those high, slashing cheekbones. The slender body outlined to perfection by her pink spandex tank and black Lycra running shorts was just icing on the cake. That, and the fact that she wasn't wearing a wedding or engagement ring.

"I think he'll be all right," she was saying with another glance at now fidgeting Davy, "but you might want to keep an eye on him for the next few hours. Watch for signs of rapid breathing, a fast heart rate or low-grade fever. All are common the first few hours after a near drowning."

Her accent was as intriguing as the rest of her. The faint lilt gave her words a different cadence. Eastern European, Mike thought, but it was too slight to pin down.

"You appear to know a lot about this kind of situation. Are you an EMT or first responder?"

"I'm a physician."

Okay, now he was doubly impressed. The woman possessed the mysterious eyes of an odalisque, the body of a temptress and the smarts of a doc. He'd hit the jackpot here. Nodding toward the colorful umbrellas just popping up at the restaurant across the highway from the beach, he made his move.

"I hope you'll let Davy and me show our appreciation by buying you breakfast, Dr. St. Sebastian."

"Thanks, but I've already had breakfast."

No way Mike was letting this gorgeous creature get away. "Dinner, then."

"I'm, uh, I'm here with my family."

"I am, too. Unfortunately." He made a face at his nephew, who giggled and returned the exaggerated grimace. "I'd be even more grateful if you give me an excuse to get away from them for a while."

"Well…"

He didn't miss her brief hesitation. Or her quick glance at *his* left hand. The white imprint of his wedding ring had long since faded. Too bad he couldn't say the same for the inner scars. Shoving the disaster of his marriage into the dark hole where it belonged, Mike overrode her apparent doubts.

"Where are you staying?"

She took her time replying. Those exotic eyes looked him up and down. Lingered for a moment on his faded T-shirt, his ragged cutoffs, his worn leather flip-flops.

"We're at the Camino del Rey," she said finally, almost reluctantly. "It's about a half mile up the beach."

Mike suppressed a smile. "I know where it is. I'll pick you up at seven-thirty." He gave his increasingly impatient nephew's shoulder a squeeze. "Say goodbye to Dr. St. Sebastian, brat."

"Bye, Dr. S'baston."

"Bye, Davy."

"See you later, Anastazia."

"Zia," she said. "I go by Zia."

"Zia. Got it."

Tipping two fingers in a farewell salute, Mike used his grip on his nephew's T-shirt to frog-walk him up the beach.

Zia tracked them as far as the row of houses on stilts fronting the beach. She couldn't believe she'd agreed to dinner with the uncle. As if she didn't have enough on her mind right now without having to make small talk with a complete stranger!

Arms folded, she watched the terrier jump and cavort alongside them. The dog's exuberance reminded her all too forcefully of the racing hound her sister-in-law had hauled down to Texas with her. Natalie was nutso over the whip-thin Magyar Agár and insisted on calling the hound Duke—much to the chagrin of Zia's brother, Dominic, who still hadn't completely adjusted to his transition from Interpol agent to Grand Duke of Karlenburgh.

The duchy of Karlenburgh had once been part of the vast Austro-Hungarian Empire but had long since ceased to exist anywhere except in history books. That hadn't stopped the paparazzi from hounding Europe's newest royal out of the shadows of undercover work. And Dom had retaliated by sweeping the woman who'd discovered he was heir to the title off her feet and into the ranks of the ever-growing St. Sebastian clan. Now Zia's family included an affectionate, übersmart sister-in-law as well as the two thoroughly delightful cousins she and Dom had met for the first time three years ago.

And, of course, Great-Aunt Charlotte. The regal, iron-spined matriarch of the St. Sebastian family and the woman who'd welcomed Zia into her home and her heart. Zia couldn't imagine how she would have made it this far in her pediatric residency without the duchess's support and encouragement.

Two and a half years, she thought as she abandoned the rest of her morning run to head back to the condo. Twenty-eight months of rounds and call rotations and team meetings and chart prep and discharge conferences. Endless days and nights agonizing over her patients. Heartbreaking hours grieving with parents while burying her own aching loss so deep it rarely crept out to haunt her anymore.

Except at moments like this. When she had to decide

whether she should continue to work with sick children for
the next thirty or forty years…or whether she should accept the offer from Dr. Roger Wilbanks, Chief of the Pedi-
atrics Advanced Research Center, to join his team. Could
she abandon the challenges and stress of hands-on medicine for the regular hours and seductive income of a world-
class, state-of-the-art research facility?

That question churned like battery acid in her gut as
she headed for the resort where the St. Sebastian clan was
staying. With the morning sun now burning bright in an
achingly blue Texas sky, the holiday sun worshippers had
begun to flock down to the beach. Umbrellas had flowered
open above rows of lounge chairs. Colorful towels were
spread on the sand, occupied by bathers with no intention
of getting wet. Patches of dead white epidermis just waiting
to be crisped showed above skimpy bikini bottoms, along
with more than one grossly distended male belly.

Without warning, Zia's mind zinged back to Mike Brennan. No distended belly there. No distended *anything.* Just
muscled shoulders and roped thighs and that killer smile.
His worn flip-flops and ragged cutoffs suggested a man
comfortable with himself in these high-dollar environs.
Zia liked that about him.

And now that she thought about it, she actually liked
the idea of having dinner with him. Maybe he offered just
what she needed. A leisurely evening away from her boisterous family. A few hours with all decisions put on hold.
A casual fling…

Whoa! Where had that come from?

She didn't indulge in casual flings. Aside from the fact
that her long hours and demanding schedule took so much
out of her, she was too careful, too responsible—all right,
just too fastidious. Except for one lamentable lapse in judgment, that is. Grimacing, she shrugged aside the memory of the handsome orthopedic surgeon who'd somehow

neglected to mention that his divorce was several light-years from being final.

She was still kicking herself for that sorry mistake when she keyed the door to the two-story, six-bedroom penthouse. Although it was still early morning, the noise level had already inched toward the top of the decibel scale. Most of that was due to her cousin Gina's almost-three-year-old twins. The lively, blue-eyed blondes acted like miniatures of their laughing, effervescent mother…most of the time. This, Zia could tell as shrieks of delight emanated from the living room, was most definitely one of those times.

An answering smile tugged at her lips as she followed the squeals to the living area. Its glass wall offered an eye-boggling panorama of the Gulf of Mexico. Not that any of the occupants of the spacious living room appeared the least interested in the view. They were totally absorbed with the twins' attempts to add blinking red Rudolph noses to the fuzzy reindeer antlers and jingle-bell halters already adorning their uncles. Dominic and Devon sat cross-legged on the floor within easy reach of the twins, while their dad, Jack, watched with diabolical delight.

"What's going on here?" Zia asked.

"Thanta's coming," curly-haired Amalia lisped excitedly. "And…"

"Uncle Dom and Dev are gonna help pull his sled," little Charlotte finished.

The girls were named for the duchess, whose full name and title filled several lines of print. Sarah's and Gina's were almost as long. Zia's, too. Try squeezing Anastazia Amalia Julianna St. Sebastian onto a computer form, she thought as she paused in the doorway to enjoy the merry scene.

No three men could be more dissimilar in appearance yet so similar in character, she decided. Jack Harris, the twins' father and the current United States Ambassador to the United Nations, was tall, tawny haired and aristocratic.

Devon Hunter's hard-fought rise from aircraft cargo handler to self-made billionaire showed in his lean face and clever eyes. And Dominic…

Ahh. Was there anyone as handsome and charismatic as the brother who'd assumed legal guardianship of Zia after their parents died? The friend and advisor who'd guided her through her turbulent teens? The highly skilled undercover agent who'd encouraged her all through college and med school, then walked away from his adrenaline-charged career for the woman he loved?

Natalie loved him, too, Zia thought with an inner smile as her glance shifted to her sister-in-law. Completely, unreservedly, joyously. One look at her face was all *anyone* needed to see the devotion in her warm brown eyes. She occupied one end of a comfortable sofa, her fingers entwined in the collar of the quivering racing hound to prevent him from joining the reindeer brigade.

Zia's cousins sat next to her. Gina, with a Santa hat perched atop her tumble of silvery blond curls and candy-cane-striped leggings, looked more like a teenager than mother of twins, the wife of a highly respected diplomat and a partner in one of NYC's most successful event-hosting enterprises. Gina's older sister, Sarah, occupied the far end of the sofa. Her palms rested lightly on her just-beginning-to-show baby bump and her elegant features showed the quiet joy of impending motherhood.

But it was the woman who sat with her back straight and her hands clasping the ebony head of her cane who caught and held Zia's eye. The Grand Duchess of Karlenburgh was a role model for any female of any age. As a young bride she'd resided in a string of castles scattered across Europe, including the one that guarded a high mountain pass on the border between Austria and Hungary. Then the Soviets invaded and later brutally suppressed an uprising by Hungarian patriots. Forced to witness her husband's execution,

Charlotte had made a daring escape by trekking over the snow-covered Alps with her newborn infant in her arms and a fortune in jewels hidden inside the baby's teddy bear. Now, more than sixty years later, she'd lost none of her dignity or courage or regal bearing. White haired and paper skinned, the indomitable duchess ruled her ever-growing family with a velvet-gloved fist.

She was the reason they were all here, spending the holidays in Texas. Charlotte hadn't complained. She considered whining a deplorable character flaw. But Zia hadn't failed to note how the vicious cold and record snowfall that blanketed New York City in early December had exacerbated the duchess's arthritis. And all it took was one mention of Zia's concern to galvanize the entire St. Sebastian clan.

In short order, Dev and Sarah had leased this six-bedroom condo and set it up as a temporary base for their Los Angeles operations. Jack and Gina had adjusted their busy schedules to enjoy a rare, prolonged holiday in South Texas. Dom and Natalie flew down, too, with the hound in tow. The family had also convinced Maria, the duchess's longtime housekeeper and companion, to enjoy an all-expenses-paid vacation while the staff here at the resort took care of everyone's needs.

Zia hadn't been able to spend quite as much time in Texas as the others. Although Mount Sinai's second- and third-year residents were allowed a full month of vacation, few if any ever strayed far from the hospital. Zia hadn't taken off more than three days in a row since she began her residency. And with the decision of whether to accept Dr. Wilbanks's offer weighing so heavily on her mind, she wouldn't have dragged herself down to Galveston for a full week if Charlotte hadn't insisted. Almost as if she'd read her mind, the duchess looked up at that moment. Her gnarled fingers tightened on the head of her cane. One snowy brow lifted in a regal arch.

* * *

Ha! Charlotte had only to look at Zia to guess what the girl was thinking! That she was so old and decrepit, she needed this bright Texas sunshine to warm her bones. Well, perhaps she did. But she also needed to put some color back into her great-niece's cheeks. She was too pale. Too thin and tired. She'd worn herself to the bone during the first two years of her residency. And worked even more the past few months. But every time Charlotte tried to probe the shadows lurking behind those weary eyes, the girl smiled and fobbed her off with the excuse that exhaustion just was part of being a third-year resident in one of the country's most prestigious medical schools.

Charlotte might not see eighty again, but she wasn't yet senile. Nor was she the least bit hesitant where the well-being of her family was concerned. None of them, Anastazia included, had the least idea that she'd engineered this sojourn in the sun. All it had taken was some not-quite-surreptitious kneading of her arthritic knuckles and one or two few valiantly disguised grimaces. Those, combined with her seemingly offhand comment that New York City felt especially cold and damp this December, had done the trick.

Her family had reacted just as she'd anticipated. Within days they'd sorted through dozens of options from Florida to California and everywhere in between. A villa on the Riviera and over-water bungalows in the South Pacific hadn't been out of the mix, either. But they'd decided on South Texas as the most convenient for both the East and West Coast family contingents. Within a week, Charlotte and Maria had been ensconced in seaside, sun-drenched luxury with various members of the family joining them for differing lengths of time.

Charlotte had even convinced Zia to take off the whole of Christmas week. The girl was still too thin and tired, but at least her cheeks had gained some color. And, the duchess noted with relief, there was something very close to a sparkle in her eyes. Even more intriguing, her glossy black hair was damp and straggly and threaded with what looked suspiciously like strands of seaweed. Intrigued, she thumped her cane on the floor to get the twins' attention.

"Charlotte, Amalia, please be quiet for a moment."

The girls' high-pitched giggles dropped a few degrees in decibel level, if not in frequency.

"Come sit beside me, Anastazia, and tell me what happened during your run on the beach."

"How do you know something happened?"

"You have kelp dangling from your ear."

Zia patted both ears to find the offending strand. "So I do," she replied, chuckling.

The lighthearted response delighted Charlotte. The girl hadn't laughed very much lately. So little, in fact, that her rippling merriment snagged the attention of every adult in the room.

"Tell us," the duchess commanded. "What happened?"

"Let's see." Playing to her suddenly attentive audience, Zia pretended to search her memory. "A little boy got sucked in by the undertow and I dove in after him. I dragged him to shore, then administered CPR."

"Dear God! Is he all right?"

"He's fine. So is his uncle, by the way. Very fine," she added with a waggle of her brows. "Which is why I agreed to have dinner with him this evening."

Two

As Zia had anticipated, the announcement that she'd agreed to dinner with a total stranger unleashed a barrage of questions. The fact that she knew nothing about him didn't sit well with the overprotective males of her family.

As a result, the whole clan just happened to be gathered for pre-dinner cocktails when the doorman buzzed that evening and announced a visitor for Dr. St. Sebastian. Zia briefly considered taking the coward's way out and slipping down to wait for Brennan in the lobby. But she figured if he couldn't withstand the combined firepower of her brother, cousins and the duchess, she might as well not waste her time with him.

She was waiting at the front door when he exited the elevator. "Hello."

"Hi, Doc."

Wow, Zia thought. Or as some of her younger patients might say, the man was chill! The easy smile was the one she remembered from this morning, but the packaging was completely different. He'd traded his cutoffs and flip-flops for black slacks creased to a knife edge, an open-necked blue oxford shirt and a casually elegant sport coat. The tooled leather boots and black Stetson were a surprise, however.

Like most Europeans, Zia had grown up on the Hollywood image of cowboys. Tom Selleck in *Last Stand at Sabre River*. Matt Damon in *All The Pretty Horses*. Kevin Costner in *Open Range*. Living in New York City for the past two and a half years hadn't altered her mental stereotype. Nor had she stumbled across many locals here in Galveston who sported the traditional Texas headgear. It looked good on Brennan, though. Natural. As though it was as much a part of him as his air of easy self-assurance and long-legged stride. It also lit a spark of unexpected delight low in her belly. The man was primo in flip-flops or cowboy boots.

She did a mental tongue-swallow and asked about his nephew. "How's Davy?"

"Sulking because he got cut off from TV and videos for the entire day as punishment for skipping out of the house."

"No aftereffects?"

"None so far. His mother's patience is wearing wire thin, though."

"I can imagine."

"My family's having drinks on the terrace. Would you like to say hello?"

"Sure."

"Be prepared," she warned. "There are a lot of them."

"No problem. My Irish grandfather married a Mexican beauty right out of a convent school here on South Padre Island. You haven't experienced big and noisy until you've been to Sunday dinner at my *abuelita*'s house."

Now that he'd mentioned his heritage, Zia could see traces of both cultures. The reddish glint in his dark chestnut hair and those emerald-green eyes hinted at the Irish in him. What she'd assumed was a deep Texas tan might well be a gift from his Mexican grandmother. Wherever the source, the combination made for a decidedly potent whole!

As she led him to the terrace that wrapped around two sides of the condo, she was glad she'd decided to dress up a bit, too. She spent most of her days in a lab coat with a stethoscope draped around her neck and her rare evenings off in comfortable sweats. She had to admit it had felt good to slither into a silky red camisole and a pair of Gina's tight, straight-leg jeans with a sparkling red crystal heart on the right rear pocket. Gina had also supplied the shoes. The lethal stilettos added three inches to Zia's own five-seven yet still didn't bring her quite to eye level with Mike Brennan.

She'd clipped her hair up in its usual neat knot, but Sarah had insisted on teasing loose a few strands to frame her face. And Dom's wife, Natalie, contributed the twisted copper torque she'd found in a London shop specializing in reproductions of ancient Celtic jewelry. Feeling like Cinderella dressed by three doting fairy godmothers, Zia slid back the glass door to the terrace.

The twelve pairs of eyes that locked on the new arrival might have intimidated a lesser man. To Brennan's credit, his stride barely faltered as he followed Zia onto the wide terrace.

"Hey, everyone," she announced. "Say hello to Mike—"

"Brennan," Dev finished on a startled note. "Aka Global Shipping Incorporated." He pushed to his feet and thrust out his hand. "How're you doing, Mike?"

"I'm good," he replied, obviously as surprised as Dev to find a familiar face at this family gathering. "You're related to Zia?"

"She and my wife, Sarah, are cousins."

"Five or six times removed," Zia added with a smile.

"The degree doesn't matter," Sarah protested. "Not among the St. Sebastians." She aimed a quizzical glance at her husband. "How do you two know each other?"

"Mike here is president and CEO of Global Shipping Incorporated, the third largest cargo container fleet in the US," Dev explained. "We contract for, what? Eight or nine million a year in long-haul shipping with GSI?"

"Closer to ten," Brennan responded.

Zia listened to the exchange in some surprise. In the space of just a few moments her sun-bronzed beach hottie had morphed to cool cowboy dude and now to corporate exec. She was still trying to adjust to the swift transitions when Dev threw in another zinger.

"And now that I think about it, doesn't your corporation own this resort? Along with another dozen or so commercial and industrial facilities in the greater Houston area?"

"We do."

"I'm guessing that's why we got such a good deal on the lease for this condo."

"We try to take care of our valued customers," Brennan acknowledged with a grin.

"Which we certainly appreciate."

Devon's positive endorsement might have carried some weight with outsiders. The two other males on the terrace preferred to form their own opinions, however. Skilled diplomat that he was, Gina's husband, Jack, hid his private assessment behind a cordial nod and handshake. Dominic was less reserved.

"Zia told us your young nephew almost drowned this morning," her brother said, his dark eyes cool. "Pretty careless of your family to let him go down to the beach alone, wasn't it?"

Brennan didn't try to dodge the bullet. A ripple of remembered terror seemed to cross his face as he nodded. "Yes, it was."

Aiming a behave-yourself glance at her brother, Zia introduced her guest to Gina, Maria and Natalie, who kept a firm hand on the collar of the lean, quivering hound eager to sniff out the new arrival. The twins regarded him from the safety of their mother's knee, but Brennan won giggles from both girls by hunkering down to their level and asking solemnly if that was a tree sprouting from Charlotte's head.

A giggling Amalia answered for her sister. "No, thilly. Those are antlers."

"Oh! I get it. She's one of Santa's reindeer."

"Yes," Charlotte confirmed as she held up two fingers, "and Santa's coming to Texas in this many days!"

"Wow, just two days, huh?"

"Yes, 'n it's our birthday, too!" She uncurled another finger. "We're going to be this many years."

"Sounds like you've got some busy days ahead. You guys better be good so you'll get lots of presents."

"We will!"

With that ringing promise producing wry smiles all around, Zia led Mike to the snowy-haired woman ensconced in a fan-backed rattan chair. He swept off his hat as Zia made the introduction.

"This is my great-aunt, Charlotte St. Sebastian, Grand Duchess of Karlenburgh."

Charlotte held out a blue-veined hand. Mike took it in a gentle grip and held it for a moment. "It's a pleasure to meet you, Duchess. And now I know why Zia's last name seemed so familiar. Wasn't there something in the papers a couple of years ago about your family recovering a long-lost painting by Caravaggio?"

"Canaletto," the duchess corrected.

Her eyelids lowered and her expression turned intensely private, as it always did when talk drifted to the Venetian landscape her husband had given her when she'd become pregnant with their first and only child.

"Would you care for an aperitif?" she asked, emerging from her brief reverie. "We can offer you whatever you wish. Or," she added blandly, "a taste of one of the finest brandies ever to come out of the Austro-Hungarian Empire."

"Say no and make a polite escape," Gina warned. "*Pálinka* is not for the faint of heart."

"I've been accused of a lot of things," Brennan responded with a crooked grin. "Being faint of heart isn't one of them."

Sarah and Gina exchanged quick, amused glances. Downing a swig of the fruity, throat-searing brandy produced only in Hungary had become something of a rite of passage for men introduced into the St. Sebastian clan. Dev and Jack had passed the test but claimed they still bore the scorch marks on their vocal chords.

"Don't say you weren't warned," Zia murmured after she'd splashed some of the amber liquid into a cut-crystal snifter.

Mike accepted the snifter with a smile. His dad and grandfather had both been hardworking, hard-living longshoremen who'd worked the Houston docks all their lives. Mike and his two brothers had skipped school more times than they could count to hang around the waterfront with them. They'd also worked holidays and summers as casuals, lashing cargo containers or spending long, backbreaking hours shoveling cargo into the holds of cavernous bulk carriers. All three Brennan sons had been offered a coveted slot in the International Longshore and Warehouse Union after they'd graduated from college. Colin and Sean had joined, but Mike had opted for a hitch in the navy instead, then used his savings and a hefty bank loan to buy his first ship—a rusty old tub that made milk runs to Central America. Twelve years and a fleet of oceangoing oil tankers and container vessels later, he could still swear and drink with the best of them.

So he tossed back a swallow of the brandy with absolute certainty that it couldn't pack half the kick of the corrosive rotgut he'd downed in and out of the navy. He knew he was wrong the instant it hit the back of his throat. He managed not to choke, but his eyes leaked like an old bucket and he had to suck air big-time though his nostrils.

"Wow!" Blinking and breathing fire, he gave the brandy a look of profound respect. "What did you say this is?" he asked the duchess between quick gasps.

"Pálinka."

"And it comes from Austria?"

"From Hungary, actually."

"Anyone ever tried to convert it to fuel? One gallon of this stuff could propel a turbocharged two-stroke diesel engine."

The smile that came into the duchess's faded blue eyes told Mike he'd survived his initial trial by fire. He wasn't ashamed to grab a ready-made excuse to dodge another test.

"I've made reservations at a restaurant just a couple of blocks from here," he told her. "Would you like to join us for dinner?" He turned to include the rest of the family. "Any of you?"

Charlotte answered for them all. "Thank you, but I'm sure Zia would prefer not to have her family regale you with stories about her misspent youth. We'll let her do that herself."

Once in the elevator, Mike propped his shoulders against the rear of the cage dropping them twenty stories. "Misspent?" he echoed. "I'm intrigued."

More than intrigued. He was as fascinated by this woman's stunning beauty as by the dark circles under her eyes. She'd tried to conceal them with makeup but the shadows were still visible, like faint bruises marring the pearly luster of her skin.

"I guess *misspent* is as good a description as any," she replied with a laugh. "But in my defense I only tried to operate on the family dog once. My brother, unfortunately, didn't get off as easily. I subjected him to all kinds of torture in the name of medicine."

"Looks like he survived okay."

He also looked decidedly less than friendly. Mike didn't blame the man. He and *his* brothers had threatened bodily harm to any male who let his glands get out of control while dating one of their sisters.

God knew Mike's glands were certainly working overtime. Despite those faint shadows under her eyes, Anastazia St. Sebastian was every man's secret fantasy come to life. Slender, graceful and so sexy she turned heads as they crossed the marble-tiled lobby and exited into the six acres of lush gardens at the center of the Camino del Rey complex.

The vacation complex was only one of several projects Mike's ever-expanding corporation had invested in to help restore Galveston after Hurricane Ike roared ashore in September 2008. The costliest hurricane in Texas history, Ike claimed more than a hundred lives and did more than $37 billion in damage all along the Gulf. Parts of Galveston were still recovering, but major investments like this beautifully landscaped luxury resort were helping that process considerably.

A frisky ocean breeze teased Zia's hair as she and Mike wound past the massive Neptune fountain the landscape architect had made the focal point of the gardens. Beyond the statue were two tall, elaborately designed wrought-iron gates that gave directly onto the beach. On the opposite side of the garden, a set of identical gates exited onto San Luis Pass Road, the main artery that ran the length of Galveston Island.

"I made reservations at Casa Mia," Mike said as he took her elbow to steer her through the gates. "Hope that's okay."

"This is my first trip to Galveston. I'm more than happy to trust the judgment of a local."

Temperatures in South Texas during the summer could give hell a run for its money. In the dead of winter, however, the balmy days and sixty-five-degree evenings were close to heaven…and perfect for strolling the wide sidewalk that bordered San Luis Pass Road. Smooth operator that he was, Mike casually shifted his hold from Zia's elbow to her forearm. Her skin was warm under his palm, her muscles firm and well-toned. He used the short walk to fill in the essential blanks. Found out she was born in Hungary. Did her undergraduate work at the University of Budapest. Graduated from medical school in Vienna at the top of her class. Had offers from a half-dozen prestigious pediatric residency programs before opting for Mount Sinai in New York City.

She elicited the same basics from him. "Texas born and bred," he admitted cheerfully. "I traveled quite a bit during my years in the navy, but this area kept pulling me back. It's home to four generations of Brennans now. My parents, grandparents, one brother and two of my three sisters all live within a few blocks of each other."

She eyed the ultraexpensive high-rises crowding the beachfront. "Here on the island?"

"No, they live in Houston. So do I, most of the time. I keep a place here on the island for the family to use, though. The kids all love the beach."

"And you're not married."

It was a statement, not a question, which told Mike she wouldn't be walking through the soft evening light with him if she had any doubts about the matter.

"I was. Didn't work out."

That masterful understatement came nowhere close to describing three months of mind-blowing sex followed by three years of growing restlessness, increasing dissatisfaction, angry complaints and, finally, corrosive bitterness. Hers, not his. By the time the marriage was finally over Mike felt as though he'd been dragged through fifty miles of Texas scrub by his heels. He'd survived, but the experience wasn't one he wanted to repeat again in this lifetime. Although...

His psyche might still be licking its wounds but his head told him marriage would be different with the right woman. Someone who appreciated the dogged determination required to build a multinational corporation from the ground up. Someone who understood that success in *any* field often meant seventy- or eighty-hour workweeks, missed vacations, opting out of a spur-of-the-moment junket to Vegas.

Someone like the leggy brunette at his side.

Mike slanted the doc a glance. One of his sisters was a nurse. He knew the demands Kathleen's career made on her and on the other professionals she worked with. Anastazia St. Sebastian had to have a core of steel to make it as far as she had.

His curiosity about the woman mounted as they turned onto a side street. A few steps later they reached the Spanish-style villa that had recently become one of Galveston's most exclusive spots. It sat behind tall gates with no sign, no lit menu box, no indication at all that it was a commercial establishment. But the hundreds of flickering votive lights in the courtyard drew a pleased gasp from Zia, and the table tucked in a private corner of the candle-lit patio was the one always made available to the top officers and favored clients of Global Shipping Incorporated.

"Back to subjecting your bother to all kinds of medical torture," he said when they'd been seated and ordered an iced tea for the doc and Vizcaya on ice for Mike, who sincerely hoped a slug of white rum would kill the lingering aftereffects of *pálinka*. "Did you always want to be a physician?"

"Always."

The reply was quick but not quite as light as she'd obviously intended. Mike hadn't survived all those summers and holidays in the bare-knuckle world of the docks without learning to pick up on every nuance, spoken or not.

"But....?" he prompted.

She flashed him a look that ran the gamut from surprised to guarded to deliberately blasé. "Med school's been a long and rather grueling slog. I'm in the homestretch now, though."

"But...?" he said again, the word soft against the clink of cutlery and buzz of conversation from other tables.

The arrival of the server with their drinks saved Zia from having to answer. She hadn't shared her insidious doubts with anyone in her family. Not even Dominic. Yet as she sipped her iced tea she felt the most absurd urge to spill her guts to this stranger.

So why *not* confide in him? Odds were she'd never see the man again after tonight. There were only a few days left on her precious vacation. And judging from Dev's comments about Global Shipping Inc., its president and CEO had a shrewd head on his shoulders. Granted, he couldn't begin to understand the demands and complexities of the medical world but that might actually be a plus. An outsider could assess her situation objectively, without the baggage of having cheered and supported and encouraged her through six and a half years of med school and residency.

"But," she said slowly, swirling the ice in her tall glass, "I'm beginning to wonder if I'm truly right for pediatric medicine."

"Why?"

She could toss out a hundred reasons. Like the overwhelming sense of responsibility for patients too young or too frightened to tell her how they hurt. The aching helplessness when faced with children beyond saving. The struggle to contain her fury at parents or guardians whose carelessness or cruelty inflicted unbelievably grievous injuries.

But the real reason, the one she'd thought she could compensate for by going into pediatric medicine, rose up to haunt her. She'd never talked about it to anyone but Dom. And even he was convinced she'd put it behind her. Yet reluctantly, inexplicably, Zia found herself detailing the old pain to Mike Brennan.

"I developed a uterine cyst my first year at university," she said, amazed that she could speak so calmly of the submucosal fibroid that had changed her life forever. "It ruptured during winter break, while I was on a ski trip in Slovenia."

She'd thought at first that she'd started her period early but the pain had become more intense with each hour. And the blood! Dear God, the blood!

"I almost died before they got me to the hospital. At that point the situation was so desperate the surgeons decided the only way to save my life was to perform an emergency hysterectomy."

She fell silent as the waiter materialized at their table to take their order. Mike sent him away with a quiet, "Give us some time."

"I love children," Zia heard herself say into the silence that followed. "I always imagined I'd have a whole brood of happy, gurgling babies. When I accepted that I would never give birth to a child of my own, I decided that at least I could help alleviate the pain and suffering of others."

"But…"

There it was. That damned "but" that had her hanging from a limb like a bird with a broken wing.

"It's hard giving so much of myself to others' children," she finished, her voice catching despite every attempt to control it. "So much harder than I ever imagined."

Her doubt and private misery filled the silence that spun out between them. Mike broke it after a moment with a question that cut to the core of her bruising inner conflict.

"What will you do if you don't practice medicine?"

"I'll stay in the medical field, but work on another side of the house."

There! She'd said it out loud for the first time. And not to her brother or Natalie or the duchess or her cousins. To a stranger, who didn't appear shocked or disappointed that she would trade her lifelong goal of treating the sick for the sterile environment of a lab.

Like all third-year residents at Mount Sinai, she'd been required to participate in a scholarly research project in addition to seeing patients, attending conferences and teaching interns. Worried by the seeming increase in hospital-acquired infections among the premature infants in the neonatal ICU, she'd searched for clues via five years' worth of medical records. Her extensive database included the infants' birth weight, ethnic origin, delivery methods, the time lapse to onset of infections, methods of treatment and mortality rates.

Although she wouldn't brief the results of her study until the much anticipated annual RRP—Residents' Research Presentation—her preliminary findings had so intrigued the hospital's director of research that he'd suggested an expanded effort that included more variables and a much larger sample base. He'd also asked Zia to conduct the two-year study under his direct supervision. If the grant came through within the next few months, she could start the research as her spring elective, then join Dr. Wilbanks's team full-time after completing her residency.

"The director of pediatric research at Mount Sinai has already asked me to join his staff," she confided to Mike.

"Is that as impressive as it sounds?"

A hint of pride snuck into her voice. "Actually, it is. Dr.

Wilbanks seems to think the study I've been working on as a resident is worth expanding into a full-fledged team effort. He also thinks it might warrant as much as a million-dollar research grant."

"That *is* impressive. What does the study involve?"

Lord, he was easy to talk to. Zia didn't usually discuss topics such as Methicillin-resistant Staphylococcus aureus, aka MRSA, with someone not wearing scrubs. Especially during a candlelit dinner.

As the incredibly scrumptious meal progressed, however, Brennan's interest stimulated her as much as his quick grasp of the essentials of her study.

She couldn't blame either his interest or his intellect for what happened when they left the restaurant, however. That was result of a lethal combination of factors. First, their decision to walk back along the beach. Zia had to remove her borrowed stilettos to keep from sinking in the sand, but the feel of it hard and damp beneath bare feet only added to her heightened perceptions. Then there was the three-quarter moon that traced a liquid silver path across the sea. And finally the arm Mike slid around her waist.

She turned into his kiss, fully anticipating that it would be pleasant. A satisfying end to an enjoyable evening. She *didn't* expect the hunger that balled in her belly when his mouth fused with hers.

He felt the kick, too. Although his hat brim shadowed his eyes when he raised his head, his skin was stretched tight across his cheeks and there was a gruff edge to his voice when he asked if she'd like to stop by his place for coffee or a drink.

Or…?

He didn't have to say it. Her pulse kicking, Zia knew the invitation was open-ended. "Don't you have company?

Davy and…" She searched her memory. "And Kevin and their mother?"

"Eileen took the kids back to town this afternoon. I suspect she won't let either of them close to the water for the next five years. She wants to thank you personally, by the way. She told me to be sure and get your phone number." Laughter rumbled in his chest. "I promised I would."

Zia hesitated for all of three seconds before digging her cell phone out of her purse. "I'll text my family and tell them not to wait up for me."

Three

The brief detour to Mike's place should have allowed plenty of time for Zia's common sense to reassert itself. *Would* have, if he hadn't taken her arm again to steer her toward a barely discernible path through the dunes. His hand was warm against her skin, his body close—too close!—to hers in the silvery moonlight.

The beach house on stilts he conducted her to was obviously new. Gleaming a pale turquoise in the moonlight, it sat on a high rise that gave it an unobstructed view of both the Gulf of Mexico and the lights of Houston gleaming in the far distance. The thick pilings looked as though they went down a mile, and white-painted storm shutters framed every window.

When Mike ushered her up the stairs to the front landing and keyed the door lock, Zia still had time to defuse the situation. Once inside, she could have drifted to the wall of windows overlooking the Gulf. Could have contemplated the moon's reflection on the dark, restless sea. Could have accepted his offer of an after-dinner brandy or coffee. Against every increasingly strident warning issued by her clinical, careful self, she ignored the view and declined a drink. Weeks of stress, indecision and near exhaustion got lost in a rush of biological need. For what was left of the night, she didn't want to think. Didn't want to do anything but give herself up to the hunger pulsing through her in slow, liquid rolls.

And Brennan didn't waste time repeating the offer. Tugging off his hat, he skimmed it carelessly toward the nearest chair and cupped her face in his palms.

"You are *so* gorgeous."

His thumbs brushed her cheeks, her lower lip. An answering need turned his forest-glade eyes as dark and restless as the sea. Zia felt another wild leap as she sensed the iron control that held him back. He was leaving it to her to dodge the bullet hurtling at them in warp speed…or step in front of it. She chose option B.

Dropping the stilettos she'd carried into the house, she hooked her arms around his neck. "So are you."

"Me? Gorgeous?" He looked startled, then amused. "Not hardly, darlin'."

The drawl came slow and rich, and the laughter in his eyes raised goose bumps of delight. That, and the quick, confident way he claimed her mouth. He was much a man, this Michael Brennan.

Very much a man, as she discovered when he lowered his hands to her waist and drew her into him. He hardened against her hip even as his lips moved over hers with dizzying skill. He'd been married, she remembered, and had learned well how to stoke a woman's fire. She was panting when he raised his head. Eager for his touch when he fumbled the clip from her hair. The heavy mass tumbled free, and Brennan buried his hands in it, holding her steady while he explored her mouth again.

With every nerve in her body alive and clamoring, Zia conducted her own avid exploration. Her palms planed his broad shoulders. Her fingers found the lapels of his sport coat. She peeled it back, forcing him to break contact long enough to wrestle free of it. He reached for her again but felt compelled to offer a gruff caveat.

"Just so you know, I don't make a habit of trying to finesse women I've just met into bed."

"Nor," she murmured, her acquired New York twang slipping away a little more with each word, "do I allow myself to be finessed."

The blood of her Magyar ancestors thrummed hot in her veins. She felt as wild as the steppes they'd swept down from on their fast, tireless ponies. As fierce as winds that howled through the mountains and valleys they'd eventually settled in.

"But tonight I shall make an exception, yes?"

"*Hell*, yes!"

He scooped her up almost before the words were out of her mouth. Cradling her against his chest, he headed in what she assumed was the direction of the bedroom. She used the short trip to attack the buttons on his crisp blue shirt.

She got the top two open and was nipping at the cords in his neck when he elbowed a door open. She gained a vague impression of wide-plank floorboards, sparse furnishings and framed posters of ships filling one wall. Then he was lowering her to a king-size bed covered in thin, buttery-soft suede.

Mike shed his shirt, boots and jeans with minimal motion and maximum speed. A real trick, considering that every drop of blood had drained from his head and was now pooled below his waist. He couldn't believe he'd managed to get the exotic, intriguing doc in his bed, but he sure as hell wasn't about to give her time for second thoughts.

Yet he dredged up enough self-control to strip her slowly, item by tantalizing item. The silky camisole. The thigh-hugging jeans with the sparkly red heart that had drawn his eyes to her butt every time she'd walked in front of him. Her half bra and thong were mere scraps of lace and easily disposed of. Then he made the near fatal mistake of pausing to drink in the sight of her long, slender curves. She gleamed like alabaster against the pearl-gray bedcover. Her hair spilled across the suede, as silky and erotic as the dark triangle at the apex of her thighs. Mike almost lost it then. Probably would have, if he hadn't gritted his teeth and held back the raging tide with the promise of exploring every slope and hollow of that luscious body.

Thank God he kept an emergency supply of condoms in the nightstand. The cache was a year old. Maybe more. With the demand for super-container ships skyrocketing and his fleet expanding almost faster than he could keep up with it, Mike hadn't had all that many opportunities to dip into this private stash. He intended to make up for those missed opportunities now, though.

If he could find the damned things! Muttering a curse under his breath, he rifled through the drawer. Where the devil had all this junk come from? With another muffled curse, he finally resorted to dumping the contents on the bed. Two dog-eared paperbacks, a handful of loose change, a spare set of keys, several socks and a plastic fire truck tumbled out.

Zia pushed up on one elbow and eyed the hook and ladder. "I've seen all kinds of sex toys during my years in med school," she said with a grin. "Some were put to rather remarkable use. But that's a new one."

"Dammit, I told Kevin and Davy to stay out... Ah! Thank God." He gave a huff of relief and held up two foil packets. "I caught the boys making water balloons out of them four or five months back but was sure I'd salvaged a few."

Four or five months back? Zia digested that little tidbit of information as he used his teeth to rip into one of the packets. Brennan must not bring many female friends to his beach house. The thought surprised her. And added another bubble to the cauldron that erupted into a furious boil at the sight of him sheathing himself.

He made quick work of it. A snap, a roll, and he tumbled her back onto the suede. He followed her down, bracing himself on his elbows to kiss her again. And again. And again. Her mouth. Her throat. Her aching breasts. Her quivering belly. When he eased a hand between her thighs, Zia went taut as a bow.

Yes! This was what she needed. What both her mind and her body craved. This wild pleasure. This dizzying spiral of excitement that contracted the muscles low in her belly. With each kiss and stroke of his busy fingers, the spasms got tighter, faster.

"Wait."

She clenched her jaw, tried to clamp down on the soaring sensations.

"Mike. Wait." She scrunched deeper into the velvety suede and reached for him. "Let me… Oh!"

Before she could do more than wrap her fingers around his rock-hard length the sensations spun into a white-hot core. Groaning, Zia gave up trying to stop the climax that shot up from her belly. She couldn't have held back if she'd wanted to. It came at her like an out-of-control freight train.

Neck arched, spine bowed, she rode it to the last shuddering sigh. When she collapsed onto the covers and opened her eyes, she saw Brennan watching her.

"Sorry," she murmured. "It's, ah, been a while."

"Oh, sweetheart." He was still hard and rampant against her hip. His shoulders were still taut, his tendons tight. Yet his grin contained nothing but smug male satisfaction. "You wouldn't be sorry if you had any idea how glorious you just looked."

Zia had studied human sexuality and the reproductive

process, of course. She could put a name to each stage of her body's response. Desire. Arousal. Lubrication. Orgasm. Satisfaction. She also knew the female of the species could generally repeat the cycle faster than the male. Still, she was surprised at *how* fast. All it took was for Mike to lean down and feather his lips over hers. The kiss was so tender—and such a contrast to the tension still locking his muscles—that Zia kicked into high gear again.

He filled her. Stroked her. Pushed her to another peak. She hung on this time and refused go over the edge without him.

Gasping and limp with pleasure, Zia knew she should get up, get dressed and go home. *Should* drifted into *later* when Mike defied conventional science by proving he could repeat the cycle after only a minimal break.

If the first round was fast and urgent, the second round was exquisitely slow. So slow, Zia had more than enough time to explore his hard, muscled body. The corded tendons, the washboard ribs, the flat belly, the five-inch scar on his left shoulder. She'd set enough stitches during her ER rotation to know a knife wound when she felt one.

"How did you get this?"

"Hmm?"

He shifted, obviously more interested her body than his own

"This scar?" she persisted. "How'd you get it?"

"It was just a slight misunderstanding."

"Between?"

"Me and a one-eyed, foul-breathed Portuguese. He was a pumper on the tanker I shipped out on the summer before my senior year in high school."

"And?"

"Let's just say Joachim didn't appreciate smart-assed

kids pointing out he hadn't grounded himself before opening the feed nozzle. Now…"

His hands cupped her butt and scooted her up a few inches.

"Let's get back to more important matters."

Zia hadn't planned to zone out. Grabbing twenty or thirty minutes to recharge in the residents' lounge had pretty much become a way of life. All she'd intended was a brief catnap between the sheets with her head nestled in the warm angle between Brennan's neck and shoulder. So when she blinked awake to a blaze of sunlight spilling through the wide windows she gave a small yelp.

"Oh, no!"

She jerked upright and pushed her hair out of her eyes. A quick glance around confirmed her hazy impressions from last night. The flooring *was* wide oak planking polished to a rich sheen. One wall *did* sport a collection of framed, poster-size photographs of oceangoing vessels. And she huddled amid a welter of silky cotton sheets topped by a cloud-soft suede cover. Naked. With what felt like a good-size patch of beard burn on her left cheek.

Oh, for heaven's sake! She was an adult. Responsible and unattached. She had no reason to feel guilty or uncomfortable about explaining a whisker scrape to her family. Or the fact that she'd spent the night with an interesting, attractive man.

A man who evidently knew his way around a kitchen. She discovered that after she'd made a trip to the bathroom, scrambled into her clothes and followed the scent of frying bacon. Mike had a small feast laid out on a glass-topped breakfast table with a breath-knocking view of the Gulf. Her surprised glance slid over the juice, sliced melon and basket of croissants to lock on a tall carafe.

With a melodramatic groan, she made her presence

known. "Please tell me that's coffee," she begged, nodding to the carafe.

Mike angled around, spatula in hand, and grinned. "It is. Help yourself."

She did, but one sip had her gasping. "Good Lord!"

"Too strong?"

"Strong doesn't begin to describe it. This makes the black tar in the resident's lounge taste good by comparison."

"Sorry. I try to remember not everyone likes navy swill. Guess I didn't water it down enough. Why don't you run another pot?"

"That's okay. I'll just doctor this one."

Several ounces of milk and two heaping spoons of sugar made the coffee marginally more palatable. Sipping cautiously, Zia leaned her hip against the marble-topped island and watched the man work. She couldn't help noting how his faded University of Texas T-shirt molded his broad shoulders and his chestnut hair showed glints of dark red in the morning sunlight. She also noticed that he wielded the spatula with easy confidence.

The bacon cooked, he drained the grease and swiped the pan with paper towels before offering her a choice. "I've got the makings for a Spanish omelet and French toast. We can do either or both."

"You don't need to go to all that trouble. I'm fine with just coffee and a roll."

"I'm not," he countered, a smile in those sexy green eyes. "We burned up the calories last night. I need sustenance. So…omelet or French toast or both?"

"Omelet. Please."

Zia settled onto one of the stools lined up at the island, a little surprised she didn't feel even a trace of morning-after awkwardness. Not that the absence should surprise her. Mike Brennan had proved an easy, attentive companion at dinner last night. She'd opened up to him about doubts and worries she hadn't even shared with Dom yet.

Which reminded her...

She'd carried her purse into the kitchen with her. She fished out her cell phone, so glad she'd sent that text last night so Dom wouldn't have the police out searching for her maimed and mutilated body. She skimmed over the list of messages and saved them to be read later before sending a brief text saying she'd be home soon. That done, she refilled her coffee cup and watched a master at work.

"Where did you learn to cook?" she asked, marveling at his chopping, browning and omelet-flipping skills.

"That one-eyed Portuguese I told you about? Joachim Caldero? He pulled doubled duty as pumper and cook. Bastard jumped ship in Venezuela. Since I was the junior crew dog aboard, the captain stuck me with galley duty." He slid the first omelet onto a plate and poured the remaining egg mixture into the frying pan. "It was either dish up canned pork and beans all the way back to Galveston or teach myself a few basic skills."

She admired the perfect half oval. "Looks like you learned more than the basics."

"I added to my repertoire over the years," he admitted with a shrug. "My ex-wife wasn't into cooking."

Or anything else that didn't involve exclusive spas and high-end boutiques. Mike didn't look back often. Nor did he wallow in regrets. But as he added diced peppers and onions to the second omelet, he had to force the memory of his soured marriage out of his head. The outing took surprisingly little effort with this stunning, dark-haired beauty watching him with admiring eyes. Playing to his audience, he flipped the omelet into a perfect crescent and let it firm before sliding it onto a plate.

"Bring your coffee," he instructed as he added bacon strips to each plate and led the way to the breakfast table.

* * *

Mike already knew he wanted more time with Dr. Anastazia St. Sebastian. Arranging a follow-up assignation turned out to be a challenge, however.

"I need to spend time with my family," she said when he proposed getting together later. "It's Christmas Eve," she added when the significance of the day failed to register with Mike.

"Oh, hell. So it is."

No way he could duck the mandatory family gathering. With its dense Hispanic concentration, the four-block area of Houston where his grandmother lived still clung to the old ways. The entire Brennan clan would gather at her house this afternoon for food and games. Come dusk, they'd troop outside to watch the traditional *posada*. Local teenagers had been chosen to portray Mary and Joseph, and the whole parish would follow with lit candles and paper lanterns.

After the procession, it was back to his *abuelita*'s to hoist the star-shaped piñata. The seven-pointed star held all kinds of religious significance, most of which Mike had forgotten. There were devils in there. He remembered that much. They had to be beaten out with a stick, with the reward being the candy that showered down on shouting, squealing kids. After that came a feast of gargantuan proportions. Tamales, *atole, buñuelos*, and *ponche*—the potent hot drink brewed from spiced fruits.

Then the Irish portion of Mike's heritage would take over. He would accompany his parents and assorted siblings to midnight Mass. Go home with them for the inevitable last-minute toy assembly and gift-wrapping. And crash until the entire clan reconvened at his parents' house Christmas morning for an orgy of present opening followed by the traditional turkey dinner.

Mike had always enjoyed the nonstop celebrations. Even when his ex-wife was at her worst. Jill had alienated everyone in the family, but she'd never managed to destroy their enjoyment in the traditions they celebrated year after year.

Tradition was one thing, Mike thought as he eyed the woman seated across the table. Anastazia St. Sebastian was another. He'd met her less than twenty-four hours ago. Still, he would cheerfully abandon any and all family rituals for a chance to spend another evening with her.

Oh, hell! Who was he kidding? He wanted more than an evening. He wanted another entire night. Or two. Three.

"What about tomorrow? After all the presents have been opened and everyone's feasted? You might need a break from the family. I know I will."

"Tomorrow's full. It's Christmas and the twins' birthday."

"The day after?"

He was pushing too hard. He knew it. But he hadn't gotten where we was today by conceding defeat without a fight. And he still had an ace in the hole.

"Actually, I have an ulterior motive for wanting to see you again."

Her inky-black brows drew together. "Ulterior?"

He could see her turning that over in her mind. Maybe wondering if she'd walked into something here. She had, but Mike didn't want to scare her off.

"Last night at dinner you told me a little about the research you're doing. I'd like to know more."

The groove in her forehead deepened. "Why?"

"GSI has an entire division dedicated to studying and implementing technological improvements. Most of our efforts focus on the petroleum and shipping industries, of course, but we've funded research in other areas, as well."

"Medical research?"

He leaned forward, all business now. "We were part of a study last year to look at the exposure of crew members to carcinogenic agents on the decks of crude oil tankers.

It assessed the effects of the lead chromate paint used in cargo holds. I've also got my people looking at ways to contain the spread of norovirus. It doesn't hit only cruise ships," he admitted wryly.

"But I'm looking specifically at MRSA and its rate of incidence in newborn infants."

"You might be interested to know two Galveston seamen sued the owners of the *Cheryl K* for two million dollars a few years back. They claimed the owners failed to inform them of an allegedly high presence of bacteria on the vessel. Both seamen became infected with MRSA."

Mike had actually forgotten about that incident until Zia mentioned the virulent virus last night. He'd hit the internet this morning, though, and was now armed with specific details.

"The men reportedly suffered multiple infections to their extremities, backs and other parts of their body. Their suit accused Cheryl K Inc. and its namesake ship of general maritime negligence, unseaworthiness and failure to pay maintenance and cure."

He'd snagged her. He saw the interest spark in her eyes and slowly, carefully reeled her in.

"If you could squeeze out an hour or so, you could talk to the head of our Support Division. He's the one who manages our technology and research divisions."

"I would love to but I fly back to New York on Friday."

"Then we'll have to do it today or tomorrow."

"You wouldn't make your man come in on Christmas Eve!"

"Actually, he's my brother-in-law. Trust me. Rafe will grab at any excuse to escape the chaos for an hour or two."

She chewed on her lower lip, obviously torn. "How about I call you after I talk to my family and see what the plans are?"

"That works." He grabbed a pen and scribbled his cell

phone number on a napkin. Once she'd tucked it in the pocket of her jeans, he pushed away from the table. "If you're ready, I'll walk you back to the resort."

"You don't need to do that."

"Sure I do." He took her hand and tugged her out of her seat. "I also need to do this."

She came into his arms so easily, so naturally. The satisfaction that gave Mike didn't come close to the jolt that hit him when she tipped her head and returned his kiss, though. The taste of her, the feel of her, raised an instant, erotic response in every part of his body. And the little purr in her throat damned near doubled him over.

He spent the entire walk back to the resort plotting ways to delay Dr. St. Sebastian's return to New York.

Four

Zia key-carded the condo's main entrance and braced herself for the inquisition ahead. To her profound relief, the male half of the St. Sebastian clan had already departed for a round of golf. The females were lingering over cups of coffee and tea before a girding up for a final shopping foray. The adult females, anyway. The twins, Gina informed Zia before she pounced, were down at the resort's kiddie playground with Maria and the hound.

"So tell us! Was Brennan as yummy in bed as he is in person?"

"Really, Eugenia." The duchess sent her granddaughter a pained look. "Do try for a little more refinement."

"Forget refinement," Sarah interjected, crossing her hands over her belly. "We want details."

Even Natalie endorsed the demand, although she prefaced it with a solemn promise *not* to share those details with Dom.

"There's not much to tell," Zia answered, grinning. *"Vidi, vici, veni."*

Despite her bubbly personality and careless tumble of curls, Gina was no dummy. She picked up immediately on the variation of Caesar's famous line and gave a hoot of delight.

"No way you're getting away with just that, Zia Mia. We need more than 'I saw, I conquered, I came.'"

"Eugenia!" The duchess issued a distinct huff. "If Anastazia wishes to explain why she spent the night with a complete stranger, she will."

"I didn't intend to," Zia admitted with a sheepish grin as she dropped into an empty chair. "We had a lovely dinner and talked about…about all kind of things."

The duchess didn't miss the brief hesitation. Charlotte cocked her head, her shrewd gaze intent on her great-niece's face, but kept silent. She disapproved of casual sex with all its inherent dangers and complications. Not that she hadn't indulged in one or two liaisons during her long years as a widow. The brief affairs couldn't erase the pain of losing her husband, of course, but they had helped to lighten it.

Just as last night appeared to have lightened some of the shadows in her great-niece's eyes. Seeing the smile that now filled them, Charlotte gave the absent Mike Brennan her silent stamp of approval.

"Then after dinner," Zia continued, "when we were walking home in the moonlight, he kissed me."

Gina pursed her lips in a long, low whistle. "That must have been some kiss."

"It was. Believe me, it was."

That produced several moments of silence, which the irrepressible Gina broke with a snicker. "So you tumbled into bed and did the happy dance. What happens now? Are you and Mike going to see each other again?"

"He wants to. But it's Christmas. Like me, he's got family obligations. And I'm flying back to New York Friday morning, so…"

"So nothing! Much as we love you, cousin of mine, we'll

understand if you decide to absent yourself for a couple of hours. Or," she added with a wicked grin, "nights."

"Thanks," Zia said wryly. "Nice to know I won't be missed. But there's no point in getting together with Mike again, as hunky as he is. He's based here in Texas, I'm in New York. For the next few months, anyway. After that…"

"After that, you'll stay in the States," Gina finished firmly. "Your family lives here. Dom and Natalie, all of us. And you're already getting offers from children's hospitals all across the country. Any of them would be lucky to have a physician with your smarts. Who knows?" she added with a gleam in her blue eyes. "You may end up here in Houston. So, yes, you should most definitely steal away with the hunk for another few hours."

To everyone's surprise, it was the duchess who settled the matter. She'd picked up on Zia's vague reference to the future and watched her face during Gina's declaration. Folding her hands on the top of her cane, she held her great-niece's gaze.

"If I've learned nothing else in my eighty plus years, Anastazia, it's that one must trust one's instincts. As you must trust yours."

She knew, Zia realized. Maybe not the exact parameters of the decision she'd been struggling with. But the duchess had obviously guessed something was weighing on her heart. Chagrined, Zia leaned over and kissed the papery skin of her cheek.

"Thank you, Aunt. I will."

Mike answered on the second ring. He didn't try to hide his satisfaction when she told him she'd like to take him up on his offer to learn more about his company's research programs.

"I can slip away for a few hours today if that doesn't mess up your plans for Christmas Eve."

"Not at all. I was just about to shut down the beach house and head into Houston. I'll pick you up."

"Then you'll have to drive all the way back out to the island."

"Not a problem."

Maybe not, but Zia had some serious showering and makeup repairs to attend to. "Also not necessary," she said firmly. "I've got a whole fleet of rental cars at my disposal. Give me the address of your corporate offices and a good time to meet you there."

Zia pulled into the underground parking lot of the steel-and-glass tower housing the corporate headquarters of Global Shipping Incorporated a little before two that afternoon. Following Mike's instructions, she found the GSI guest parking slots and took the elevator to the three-story lobby dominated by a monster Christmas tree. Bubbling fountains and a rippling stream cut through a good half acre of marble tile, serenading her as she checked in at the security desk.

The uniformed guard wished her happy holidays and checked her ID. "I'll let Mr. Brennan know you're here," he said, handing her a bar-coded guest pass. "Take the first elevator on the left. It'll shoot you right to the GSI offices."

"Thanks."

The express elevator opened to a reception area with an eagle's-eye view of the Houston skyline. An electronic map of the world took up one entire wall, with flashing lights designating GSI's ships at sea. Zia's eyes widened at the array of green and amber dots. The legend beside the map tagged the green dots as cargo ships and the amber ones as oil tankers.

She was trying to guesstimate the total number when Mike emerged from an inner office accompanied by the individual she presumed was his brother-in-law. Both wore jeans and open-necked shirts but the similarity stopped there. Where Mike was tall, tanned and green-eyed, the man with him had jet-black hair, a pencil-thin mustache and a smile that emitted at least a thousand kilowatts of wow-power.

"Hello, Zia."

They strode forward to greet her, presenting a double whammy of pure masculinity.

"This is Rafe Montoya, GSI's VP for Support Systems. The poor guy's married to my sister Kathleen."

"It's a pleasure to meet you, Dr. St. Sebastian."

"Please, call me Zia."

"Zia it is." He took her hand in both of hers. "The whole family's still shaken over Davy's near miss yesterday. You have our deepest gratitude."

"I'm just glad I was there."

"So are we." Releasing her hand, he cut right to the reason they'd congregated in the empty office building. "I understand you're an expert in bacterial infections."

"Not an expert, by any means, but I'm compiling statistical data on the increasing incidence of infectious diseases in newborn infants."

"A disturbing trend, certainly. As is the increasing incidence of both bacterial and viral infections among crews at sea. Would you like to see some of the data we've collected?"

"Very much."

"I set up my laptop in Miguel's office."

"Miguel?" she echoed as Mike gestured to the set of double doors leading to the inner sanctum.

"Miguel, Mick, Mickey, Mike, Michael. I answer to any and all."

"Don't forget your sisters' favorite," his brother-in-law interjected, pitching his voice to a reedy falsetto. "Mike-eee."

With a good-natured grimace, Mike-eee ushered her

into a spacious, light-filled office. It was surprisingly un-cluttered. The desk was a slab of acrylic on twin, bow-shaped arcs of bronze. A matching conference table was positioned beside the windows to take advantage of the distant view of Houston's busy docks. Above the credenza that ran the length of one wall was another map, this one depicting global shipping lanes. The computer-generated routes crisscrossed cobalt-blue oceans in a spaghetti tangle of neon red, gold, green and black.

Zia noted with interest the eclectic collection of items Mike had obviously picked up in his travels. An elaborately carved boomerang that looked big enough to take down an elephant occupied a triangular frame made of some exotic wood. A three-foot-high Maori tiki god painted persim-mon red sat on a pedestal, his face screwed into a ferocious grimace and his tongue stuck out, presumably to deride would-be enemies. And standing in a corner like a fourth attendant at the meeting was a tan canvas dive suit topped by a dented brass helmet.

"I made coffee," Mike told Zia, "but there's tea or soft drinks or water if you'd prefer."

"Water would be great, thanks."

"Wise decision," Montoya commented as he powered up his computer. "Miguel's coffee has the flavor and con-sistency of bilge water."

"I had a sample this morning," Zia replied, laughing. "It would certainly rank up there with some of the bile we resi-dents down to stay awake during a thirty-six-hour rotation."

Montoya hiked a brow but he was too well mannered to follow up on her admission that she'd shared morning coffee with his brother-in-law. Instead, he tapped a couple keys on his laptop. The computerized wall map faded to a blank screen.

"As you can imagine, the health of the crews that man our ships is an ongoing concern. The IMO—International

Maritime Organization—has set guidelines for conducting pre-sea and periodic fitness examinations for all crewmembers. Despite this medical screening, however, we've noted disturbing trends in recent years.

"Part of that stems from the fact that seamen constitute a unique occupational group. Their travel to different parts of the world exposes them to infections and diseases at a rate comparable only to that of airline crews. And, like airline crews, they generally remain in port for relatively short time periods."

"But wouldn't a short turnaround mitigate their risk of exposure?"

"You'd think so, but that doesn't prove to be the case. In fact, seafarers report an incidence of certain diseases eight to ten times higher than the international average."

Montoya brought up the first slide. Its no-nonsense title—Infectious Diseases—riveted Zia's attention instantly.

"GSI maintains a database of all medical issues that impact our crews, but I extracted the data Mike indicated you might be particularly interested in."

The title slide gave way to a series of graphs that tracked GSI's reported incidents of HIV, malaria, hepatitis A, B and C, and tuberculosis against the international average. As Montoya had warned, the numbers were significantly higher than those Zia was familiar with.

"Although GSI is below the maritime average in every category, we're concerned by the worldwide upward trend in both malaria and tuberculosis. As a result we've funded or contributed heavily to a number of research projects targeting those diseases."

The next slide listed five studies, the company or institute that conducted them and the dollars GSI had contributed. The string of 0's on each study made Zia blink.

"Mike said you're focusing specifically on MRSA-related incidents," Montoya commented.

"That's right."

"We track that data, too."

She leaned forward, her interest riveted once again as he brought up the next slide. It showed the number of MRSA incidents by year and then by ship.

"Damn," Zia muttered. "You're seeing an across-the-board increase, too."

"Unfortunately."

"That's one nasty bug," Mike put in.

"Yes, it is. And becoming more and more resistant to antibiotics."

"Which is why we'd be interested in the results of your study," Montoya continued.

Startled, Zia started to protest that she'd focused on the very controlled world of neonatal nurseries. She couldn't imagine an environment farther removed from a massive container ship or oil tanker until she stopped, backed up and thought about it for a moment. The grim fact was that MRSA was on the rise in hospitals, nursing homes, homeless shelters, military barracks and prisons. All places where people were crowded and confined. Crews on ocean-going vessels certainly fell into that category.

"I'd be more than happy to share my findings, as limited as they are."

GSI's chief executive officer and VP for Support Systems exchanged a glance.

"Mike mentioned the possibility you might expand your research," Montoya said. "If so, GSI might be in a position to help with a grant."

Zia's jaw sagged. No way she would have imagined that a casual dinner date with a near stranger could lead to funding for the kind of in-depth study Dr. Wilbanks had talked to her about.

"Are you serious?"

"Very much so. We'd have to see a proposal that includes

all the standard criteria, of course." He ticked them off with knowledgeable ease. "A comprehensive rationale for the study. An assessment of the resources required. A detailed budget for the initial start-up, along with an estimated budget for the entire project. Biographical sketches of the people on your team, what you hope to accomplish and so on."

"Right."

Her mind whirled. Global Shipping Inc. had just made the question of whether she should switch from hands-on medicine to research ten times more difficult. Up to this point the possibility of participating in a major research effort with big-dollar funding had been just that—a possibility. Suddenly it had moved into the realm of probable. *If* she chose to go in that direction.

"Would you make me copies of these slides?"

She needed to study the data and think about the possibility of cross-fertilization with her research.

"Certainly."

He hit a key on his laptop. A sudden whir sounded from the printer on the sleek credenza behind Mike's desk. While he went to retrieve the copies, Montoya extracted a slim case from his shirt pocket.

"Here's my card. Please let me know if and when you're ready to put your proposal together. I'll be happy to take a look at it and provide input from this end."

Zia nodded, her mind still churning, and slipped his business card into her purse.

"Now, if you'll excuse me, I'd better get back to *abuelita*'s before the kids have Kate pulling out her hair." He shut down the laptop and tucked it under his arm. "It was good meeting you, Zia. Mike explained that you're pressed for time, but if you can squeeze out another hour or two I know the rest of the family would like to meet you, too."

"Particularly Davy's mom," Mike added. "Eileen called

just before you arrived with explicit instructions to bring you by the house if at all possible."

"Well…"

Zia checked her watch, surprised to find the session with Rafe Montoya had lasted a mere forty minutes.

Sarah, Gina and Natalie hadn't left to go shopping until almost noon. They'd taken the twins with them to give Maria and the duchess some downtime. Zia suspected both women were on the balcony, their feet up and eyes closed for an afternoon snooze.

The men would have finished their golf game by now but would no doubt hit the clubhouse before returning to the condo. Nothing formal was planned until this evening, when the family would follow the age-old Hungarian custom of celebrating *Szent-este*, or Holy Evening, with carols and a Bethlehem play using nativity figures.

Once the girls were in bed, the adults would indulge in a little stronger Christmas Eve cheer. Tomorrow would bring church services, the extravagant Christmas buffet at the resort's tony restaurant and the twins' birthday party later in the day. If Zia was going to meet the other members of the Brennan family, it had to be this afternoon.

"I guess I could stop by for a quick visit," she told Mike.

"Great." He grabbed his hat and settled it low on his forehead. "Everyone's congregated at our grandmother's house. It's only a few miles from here."

"I'll follow you."

Those few miles took them out of the canyon of downtown skyscrapers into what was once obviously a working-class neighborhood of small stucco houses. Property values must be shooting up, though, as newer and much larger residences appeared to be replacing the older homes.

Red, pink and white oleander bushes defined front- and backyards, while hundred-year-old live oaks dripping with

Spanish moss formed dense canopies. A heavy Hispanic flavor showed in storefront signs and churches with names like Our Lady of Guadalupe and Saint Juan Diego. Mike turned onto a tree-lined street and pulled up behind a string of vehicles parked curbside in the middle of the block. Zia parked behind him and got out, careful to avoid a hot-pink bike lying on its side in the middle of the sidewalk.

"This'll be Teresa's," Mike said as he whisked the bike up and out of the way. "She's Davy and Kevin's sister and the bane of their existence, the way they tell it. Here, let's go around to the patio. Everyone's usually out back."

As they followed a winding path, Zia admired the skillful way the original one-story stucco house had been expanded. The stone-fronted second story added both living space and architectural interest, while a glassed-in sunroom extended the first floor and brought the outdoors in.

"Does your grandmother live here alone?"

"She did until recently. My youngest sister and her new baby have moved in while her husband's in Afghanistan. We're negotiating with *abuelita* what'll happen when Maureen moves back out."

"How many brothers and sisters do you have again?"

"Three sisters, three brothers. Between them they've produced fifteen offspring...so far. And from the sound of it," he added, cocking his head as high-pitched shrieks of laughter emanated from the rear of the house, "they're pretty much all here."

Even with that warning, the noise and sheer size of the crowd in the backyard made Zia blink. Three little girls clambered in and out of a plastic castle while two others and a toddler made good use of a swing set. Several boys of varying ages played a game of tag with two joyously barking dogs. One was a large mixed breed, the other the small wirehaired terrier Zia remembered from yesterday morning. His owner, Davy, appeared to be suffering no aftereffects from his dunking as he raced after an older, near carbon copy, who had to be his brother, Kevin.

Additional family members crowded the glass-topped tables and lounge chairs set under a pergola draped with red and green lanterns. Kids occupied one table, adults another, both groups involved in noisy board games. The rhythmic beat of "Feliz Navidad" rose above the dogs' barking, shrieks of laughter and buzz of conversation. The music pulsed through a screen door that must lead to the kitchen, Zia guessed as she breathed in the tantalizing scents of roasting pork and spicy chipotle marinade.

One of the board players glanced up and caught sight of the newcomers. Pushing away from the table, the brunette jumped out of her chair and rushed across the lawn.

"Mike called and said you were stopping by, Dr. St. Sebastian. Thank you!" Disdaining formalities, she enveloped Zia in a fierce hug. "Thank you so much!"

"I'm just glad I was in the right place at the right time."

"Me, too! I'm Eileen, by the way. Eileen Rogers."

"And this is her husband, Bill," Mike said, introducing yet another of his brothers-in-law. This one didn't come anywhere close to either Mike *or* Rafael Montoya on the hotness index, but his warm brown eyes signaled both sincerity and a keen intelligence.

"You have my thanks, too, Dr. St. Sebastian. From the bottom of my heart."

"You're welcome. Both of you. And please, call me Zia."

"That's short for Anastazia, right?" Eileen hooked arms with her son's rescuer. "I looked you up on the internet," she admitted as she tugged Zia toward the others. "You're Hungarian, graduated from med school in Vienna and are just about to finish a residency at Mount Sinai."

"I think Zia knows her pedigree," Mike drawled from behind them.

Eileen ignored him. "You're also the sister of the yummy

Grand Duke of Karlenburgh, whose face was plastered all over the tabloids last year. Kate, Maureen and I all drooled over his picture."

"Thanks," her husband said with a mock groan. "Just what the rest of us mere mortals needed to hear."

His comment almost got lost in a chorus of excited shouts. The kids—all ten or twelve or fifteen of them—had noticed the newcomers' arrival. Like a human tsunami, they surged past Zia and Eileen emitting shrill squeals.

"Uncle Mickey! Uncle Mickey!"

They swamped him. Literally. Hung on his arms and wrapped around his legs. He crab-walked past the two women with kids dangling from every extremity. Zia laughed, but Eileen's chuckle ended on a low, almost inaudible mutter.

"Damn that bitch."

Zia sent her a startled glance. "Excuse me?"

"Sorry." Color rushed into the other woman's cheeks. "I shouldn't have let that slip out. It's just…"

"Just what?"

Eileen bit her lip, her gaze on the shrieking tangle of humanity a few yards ahead. "Mike is so good with them. With all of them. He'd make such a fantastic father."

A sudden, queasy sensation hit Zia. She had a feeling she knew where this was going. Her stomach muscles clenched, preparing to ward off the blow that Eileen Rogers delivered like a roundhouse punch.

"I probably shouldn't air our family's dirty laundry, but…" Eileen's voice flattened. Hardened. "It broke our hearts when his bitch of an ex-wife announced she didn't want children. Broke Mike's heart, too, although he would never admit it."

Five

Mike could sense the change in Zia. The signs were subtle—a slight dimming of the smile in her exotic eyes, just a hint of reserve in her responses to his family's boisterous welcome. He shouldn't have been surprised, given how many there were of them!

Interesting, though, that he'd become so attuned to this woman's small nuances after only one night together. He did his best to wipe the erotic mental images out of his head as he introduced her around. Her every move got to him, though. Each time she hooked a strand of hair behind her ear or bent to catch something someone said or just glanced his way, Mike felt a tug. And each tug only increased his determination to get to know Anastazia St. Sebastian a whole lot better.

She renewed her acquaintance with Davy and his terrier before Mike introduced her to his parents. He could see her relaxing a little as they welcomed her. It would be hard not to relax around Eleanor and Big Mike Brennan, given that they were two of the most unpretentious and genuine people on God's green earth. And, of course, Zia had snatched their grandson from the treacherous waters of the Gulf. That put her right at the top of their list of can-do-no-wrong human beings.

The shamrock-green eyes Big Mike had passed to six of his seven of his children beamed his gratitude. "You need anything, Doc, anything at all, you just call. What Mickey here can't do for you, Eleanor or I or one of the others will."

Zia looked a little overwhelmed by the offer but accepted it graciously. "Thank you."

She connected with Mike's middle sister, too. Not surprising, since the two women shared a common bond. Jiggling her nine-month-old on her hip, Kate expanded on that link. "I don't know if Mickey told you that I'm a cardiovascular surgical nurse at St. Luke's, here in Houston."

"He mentioned that you're a nurse, but not your specialty. Cardio's a tough area."

"It can be," Kate admitted cheerfully. "My husband, Rafe, said you're doing a research study on MRSA. Obviously, I have a vested interest in hospital-acquired infections. I'd love to sit down and talk with you about your study sometime. Maybe we could do lunch after the craziness of the holidays?"

"I wish we could. Unfortunately, I'm flying home to New York the day after tomorrow."

"Too bad." Her gaze turned speculative. "My brother hasn't shown much interest in any of the women Eileen and Mo and I have thrown at him the past three years. Not enough to bring them home to meet the family, anyway. You've obviously made an impression."

"Obviously," Mike's youngest sister chimed in, joining the group. Like Kate and most of the other Brennan siblings, Maureen had inherited their father's shimmering green eyes, but her red hair was at least a dozen shades lighter and brighter than the others'.

As though uncomfortable with the turn the conversation had taken, Zia smiled and redirected it. "I understand your husband's in the military."

"That's right. He's army, despite Colin and Mickey's attempt to browbeat him into going navy."

"Colin being the most obnoxious of my brothers," Mike warned with a grin as he shepherded Zia toward the men waiting their turn. "Right after Sean and Dennis."

He made quick work of the intros to the rest of the clan. Brothers, sisters-in-law, kids all got a brief acknowledgment before Mike whisked Zia away to meet the clan's matriarch.

Consuela Brennan's unlined skin and calm black eyes belied her age. To Mike's admittedly biased minds, his grandmother still exuded an aura of quiet beauty and the convent-bred serenity that had captivated his rough-and-tumble Irish grandfather so many years ago.

"So you are the one who saved our little Davy." She framed Zia's face with her palms. "I lit a candle this morning to thank God for His grace in bringing you into our lives. I will light another each day for a year."

"I…uh…thank you."

"And now, I think, you should sit here in the shade with Eleanor and me and tell us about your country. Miguel says you're from Hungary. I must confess I know little about it."

Zia chatted with Consuelo and Eleanor Brennan for a good twenty minutes or more. The mother- and daughter-in-law were very different in both age and interests but shared an absolute devotion to each other and to their families. Under any other circumstances, Zia would have thoroughly enjoyed getting to know them better.

Yet she couldn't help sneaking an occasional side glance, observing Mike interact with his siblings and in-laws. Noting, as well, how his nieces and nephews all seemed to adore him. Cries of "Uncle Mickey, watch me!" and "Come push me, Uncle Mickey!" peppered the air. Each shout, every giggle and squeal of delight, seemed to reinforce his sister Eileen's earlier comment. Mike Brennan would make a fantastic father.

The thought twisted like a small knife in Zia's chest. She shrugged the familiar pain aside as she said her goodbyes and wished everyone merry Christmas but it was still there, buried deep, as Mike walked her to her car.

"You have a wonderful family," she said, smiling to cover the ache. "I thought mine was big and lively, but yours wins the prize."

"They keep life interesting."

She fished out the keys of the rental and clicked the lock, but Mike angled between her and the door.

"I want to see you again, Zia. Sure you can't slip away again tonight or tomorrow?"

She wanted to. God, she wanted to! With him leaning so close, his smile crinkling the tanned skin at the corners of his eyes, his body almost touching hers, all she could think of was how his hands had stroked her. How he'd kissed and teased and tormented her. How she'd given more of herself to this man in one night than she'd ever given before.

She had a sneaking suspicion she could fall in love him. So easily. He was smart, handsome, fun, unpretentious and devoted to his family...which was the one thing she *couldn't* give him.

"I'm sorry, Mike. I need to spend tonight with my family. And tomorrow isn't just Christmas, it's also the twins' birthday. Gina wants to make a big deal of it since the girls won't have any of their friends from preschool to play games and blow out candles with, so we'll all be doubly..."

He laid a finger on her lips. "Leave it to me. I'll find a way to make it happen."

Not if she didn't answer her phone or return his calls. Trying to convince herself it was better to cut the cord now, before they got in any deeper, Zia shook her head. "Best to just say goodbye now."

He looked ready to argue the point but gave in with a shrug.

"Okay."

Bending, he brushed his lips over hers. The first pass was light, friendly. The second set her heart thumping against her sternum.

"Goodbye, Zia. For now."

He didn't call to press the issue. Although Zia had made up her mind to end things between them before they could really get started, she had to admit she was surprised. Okay, maybe a little miffed.

She spent Christmas Eve enjoying the twins' almost giddy eagerness over Santa's imminent arrival and the fact that they would share their birthday with Baby Jesus the next day.

The evening blended so many traditions, old and new. With her eye for color and genius for party planning, Gina made the most of all of them. The tree, the carols, the twins' construction-paper daisy chains draped like garlands at the windows. Stockings hooked above the marble fireplace for every member of the family, the hound included. White candles giving off just enough heat to gently turn the five-tiered nativity carousel, a reminder of the duchess's Austrian roots and a precious memento from Sarah and Gina's childhood.

They celebrated the Hungarian side of the St. Sebastian heritage, as well. Zia and Natalie spent a fun hour in the kitchen baking *kiffles*, the traditional Hungarian cookie made from cream cheese dough and filled with various flavors of pastry filling. Delicate and sinfully rich, they made a colorful holiday platter in addition to supplying the required treat to leave for Santa.

The highlight of the evening was the Bethlehem play orchestrated by Zia and Dom. The original folk tradition went back centuries, when children dressed in nativity costumes would go from house to house. Carrying a crèche, the young shepherds and wise men accompanying Joseph and Mary would sing and dance choreographed versions of the birth of Christ. Their performance would be rewarded with a treat of some kind at each house.

The tradition had gone through many different variations over the centuries. Most Bethlehem plays these days were performed at churches or schools. So Dom and Zia had to improvise costumes and staging and conscript the other adults for various roles. The performance delighted the twins, however. So much so that everyone was exhausted by the time Gina and Jack finally got them to bed.

The next morning the hyper-excited twins roused everyone before seven, the hound included. Gina and Jack were determined the girls should experience all the joy of Christmas morning, so their follow-up birthday celebration wasn't planned until late that afternoon…a timetable Mike Brennan exploited very nicely.

The call came after the family returned from church services and had all trooped down to the resort's elegant restaurant for the Christmas buffet. They were waiting to be seated when Dev's cell phone pinged. He checked caller ID and shot Zia a glance before answering.

"Hey, Brennan. What's happening?" He listened a moment, his brow hiking. "Yeah, she's right here."

To everyone's surprise, he handed the phone to Gina instead of Zia. She took it with a bewildered look. "Hi, Mike. Yes," she said after a brief pause. "Around four."

Another pause, punctuated by a wide smile.

"The twins would love that! If you're sure it's not too

much trouble. Yes. Yes, by all means! Great! We'll see you then."

Grinning, she hung up and addressed a phalanx of questioning faces. Her brightest smile went to Zia. "How sweet of you to tell Mike that you couldn't pass up the girls' birthday party to see him again."

"I…well…"

"So he's coming to the party," she said happily. "With a piñata and a pony and a half-dozen nieces and nephews, all close to the girls' age. He said he knew the twins' friends were all back home, so he thought they might like to share their special day with new ones."

Zia could only stare at her, openmouthed, and left it to the girls' father to inquire drily how they were supposed to accommodate a pony in the condo.

"Mike suggested we have the party in the play area. He's already spoken to the resort manager. The entire playground is ours for the duration." She hunkered down to address her wide-eyed daughters. "What do you say, girls? Do you want pony rides and a piñata at your party?"

Amalia stamped both feet and clapped her hands enthusiastically. "Yeth!"

Wide-eyed, serious Charlotte had to ask, "What's a piñata?"

By six-thirty that evening, Zia's suspicion that she could fall in love with Mike Brennan had solidified into certainty. She'd never met any man more suited to a brood of nosy, lively children. Children she could never give him, she reminded herself with a slice of pain.

And then, when the last of the kids had driven off with their respective parents and Zia's family had retreated to the condo, it was just her. Just him.

The salt breeze fluttered the ruffles of the cinnamon-colored overblouse she'd changed into along with jeans and a pair of sandals more suitable to a playground party. Mike had changed, too, and was once again in his beach persona of shorts and flip-flops. Trying to decide which version she liked best, Zia ached to lose herself in the smile she saw in his eyes.

"Thank you. You made this day so special for the twins. For all of us."

"It's not over yet." He tilted his head toward the surf rustling against the deserted shoreline. "Walk with me?"

Zia's precise mind tabulated an instant list of reasons not to let this man burrow deeper into her heart. Just as quickly, she countered them with the same arguments she'd trotted out yesterday. She was leaving tomorrow. Flying back to cold, snowy New York. She'd most likely never see him again. Why not make the most of these stolen hours?

"Sure."

As they tracked a path of side-by-side footsteps in the damp sand, his hand folded around hers. His grip remained loose, his voice easy as they swapped stories from their childhood and tales of Christmases past. By contrast, a tight, delicious tension gathered in the pit of Zia's stomach. It had knotted into a quivering bundle of need by the time the pale turquoise silhouette rose above the dunes directly ahead.

"I know you must be tired," Mike said as they approached the beach house, "but I don't want the day to end. How about we have that drink I offered last night but we never quite got around to?"

"A drink sounds good."

He'd closed the shutters after Zia had left yesterday morning. No light spilled through them as they took the path through the dunes and mounted the zigzagging staircase. Once inside the beach house, she sniffed the faint scent of trapped salt air. Mike made quick work of folding back the shutters protecting the French doors in the high-ceilinged living room, though, and opened them to let in the sea breeze.

"Would you like coffee or something a little stronger?"

"No offense, but your coffee should be registered with the EPA as a class II corrosive."

"True." Grinning, he acknowledged the hit. "But ironic coming from the woman whose great-aunt serves *pálinka* to unsuspecting guests."

"I tried to warn you."

"Yeah, you did. I think I have a less explosive brandy."

The banter was relaxed, the Courvoisier he poured into two snifters as smooth as sin. And with each sip, the need to touch him grew more critical. She fought the urge, determined to stretch their time together for as long as possible, and carried her drink out to the deck.

The wraparound, multilevel deck was banded by a railing of split boards spaced close enough to keep young nieces and nephews from wiggling through and plunging to the dunes below. The top rail was wide and flat and set at just the right height for adults to lean their elbows on. Zia took advantage of the ledge, cradling the heavy snifter in both hands while she absorbed the vista of foaming surf and the sky purpling out over the Gulf.

"You know," Mike mused as his elbows joined hers on the weathered shelf, "the NMC is working on a program that would allow mariners to upgrade or renew their credentials on demand from any cyber location in the world."

She angled to face him, not sure where he was going with that conversational gambit. "NMC?"

"Sorry. The National Maritime Center. It's a US Coast Guard agency, under the auspices of the Department of Homeland Security. The center is responsible for credentialing US mariners. The process is complicated and time-consuming now, but the NMC's new program would let crews access the system electronically, just like they access their bank accounts or withdraw cash from an ATM."

"Sounds reasonable."

"GSI provided input into the initial system architecture."

"Oh-kay."

She still couldn't guess where this was heading, especially with the swiftly falling darkness painting Mike's face in shadows.

"NMC's presenting a status update briefing at the Maritime Trades Association's executive board meeting in mid-January. I was supposed to be in Helsinki and hadn't planned to attend but now I'm thinking I might. The meeting's in New York. Not," he added with an exaggerated drawl, "that I need an excuse to come callin'."

She wasn't expecting the sudden zing of excitement at the prospect of seeing him again. It took every ounce of Zia's resolve to squelch it.

"I've enjoyed our time together, Mike, as brief as it's been. But…" She pulled in a breath. "I don't think it's a good idea for us to try to build on it."

"Funny, I think it's a hell of an idea."

She had a dozen convenient excuses she could have thrown out. She was supervising four interns, conducting team meetings, examining patients, doing chart reviews— and all this less than two weeks away from presenting the results of her research study. She also owed Dr. Wilbanks an answer when she got back to New York.

But dealing with patients and anxious relatives had taught Zia it was best to be honest. She usually softened a harsh truth with sympathy, but sometimes it was stark and unavoidable. This was one of those times.

"I like you, Mike. Too much to let either of us get in over our heads."

"Okay, that needs a little more explaining."

"The other evening, during dinner, I told you about… about the skiing trip in Slovenia that ended in disaster."

Now it was his turn to look as though he wasn't sure where the conversation was going. "I remember."

"I watched you with your family yesterday. With my family today. You're so good with the children." She dragged in another breath and carefully centered her snifter on the broad ledge. "You don't need to get involved with a woman—*another* woman—who isn't going to give you any."

"Well, Christ! Which one of my loving sisters told you about…?" He shook his head, exasperated. "Never mind. It doesn't matter. What does matter is that we're a long ways yet from getting in over our heads."

"Which is why I say…" She caught her accent slipping and forced a correction. "Why I *said* we should stop now, before either of us gets hurt."

He angled his head, studying her in the deepening twilight. She couldn't see the expression in his eyes, only the purse of his lips as he weighed her comment.

"How about we strike a deal here?" he said after several long moments. "I'll tell you if and when I approach the hurting stage, and you do the same."

Rendben! Oké! She'd warned him. Made it perfectly clear they could never become serious. So…

"All right."

"All right?"

"I accept the deal." She hooked a hand behind his neck, tugged him down to her level. "And just to seal the bargain…"

Mike was careful not to let his quick, visceral triumph flavor the kiss. He hadn't lied. He *was* a long way yet from getting in over his head. But he was navigating in that direction and had no intention of charting a different course. Zia St. Sebastian fascinated and challenged and aroused him in ways he hadn't been fascinated or challenged or aroused in a long, long time.

Her revelation the other night at the restaurant that she couldn't have children had given him pause for maybe ten, fifteen seconds. It had also brought back some bitter memories. Right up until he reminded himself there was a whole passel of difference between *couldn't* and *wouldn't*.

Zia wasn't Jill. The two women might have been bred on different planets. Different universes. And right now, all Mike wanted to do was revel in those differences. Like the way Zia's mouth molded his with no coy pretense of having to be coaxed. The fit of her tall, slender body against his, so perfect he didn't have to stoop or contort to cant her hips into his. The lemony scent of her shampoo, the smoky taste of Courvoisier on her lips, the way the skin at the small of her back warmed under his searching fingers when he tugged up the hem of her blouse. Every touch, every sensory signal that raced along his snapping nerves, made him raw with wanting her.

He managed to keep from tugging the ruffled blouse over her head and baring her to the night. But he did circle her waist and perch her on the wide ledge. The move put her nose just a few inches above his and gave him easy access to the underside of her chin.

"You know," he said as he nibbled the tender skin, "you're a hard woman to please. I had to call a dozen stables before I found someone who would deliver a pony this afternoon."

"That was your idea, not mine," she reminded him, threading her fingers through his hair. "And totally unnecessary, I might add. The piñata and kids were more than enough. But I appreciate the trouble you went to."

"Yeah, well, since you brought it up…"

"*You* brought it up."

"I'm talking about your appreciation."

"Is that right?" She used her hold on his hair to tilt his head back. "What about it?"

"Well, it just seems to me there are a number of ways you might show it."

Her eyes glinted with amusement. "Just what did you have in mind, cowboy?"

He answered her question with a quick barrage of his own. "What time's your flight tomorrow?"

"Eleven-twenty."

"From Houston Hobby or George Bush Intercontinental?"

"Houston Hobby."

"And how long will it take you to pack?"

"Thirty minutes. Maybe less. *Why*?"

"Hold on." He settled his hands on her hips and pretended to conduct a series of rapid mental calculations. "Okay, the way I figure it we have fifteen and a half hours. Should be just enough time for me to go through my entire repertoire of moves and send you back to New York a happy woman."

"Good Lord!" The amusement bubbled into laughter. "Fifteen and a half hours going through your repertoires and I won't be able to walk, much less board a plane."

Which was pretty much the idea. Mike didn't share that thought, choosing instead to scoop her off the rail and into his arms.

"Better call back to the condo," he suggested as he carried her, still grinning, into the house. "Your brother wasn't looking all that friendly this afternoon."

"Are you worried what Dom might think?"

"More what he might do," Mike admitted wryly. "Which is probably exactly the same thing I would if any of *my* sisters spent fifteen and a half hours engaged in the kind of activity I have planned for you, Doc."

Six

Zia slept for the entire flight from Houston to LaGuardia. Hardly a surprise, given that Mike had made good on his promise to keep her busy for an astonishing portion of their stolen interlude.

When she exited the terminal, the icy air hit like a slap in the face. Luckily, she'd worn her UGGs and fleece-lined parka on the flight down to Texas. They protected her now while she stood in the taxi line, but the howling wind sliced into the tiger-striped leggings Gina had given her for Christmas and her nose dripped like a faucet by the time she tumbled into a cab.

After a week of sun-washed beaches and balmy days, the dirty slush and nasty gray sky should have been a shock to her system. Yet as the taxi rattled over the Robert F. Kennedy Bridge and headed for Manhattan's Upper West Side, the hustle and bustle of her adopted city grabbed her. She loved its pulsing rhythm, its cultural diversity, its kitsch and class. Of course, her perceptions were skewed by the fact that she now lived in one of the city's most famous apartment buildings.

As the cab pulled up at the entrance to the Dakota, Zia couldn't help thinking how much the multistory Victorian-era complex reminded her of her native Budapest. Gabled and fancifully turreted, the Dakota stood out from the modern structures crowding it on three sides and drew the eye with the same regal dignity as the iconic spires of Hungary's parliament building.

Charlotte St. Sebastian had purchased her fifth-floor, seven-room apartment after an odyssey that included her escape from the Soviets and short stays in both Vienna and Paris. Her title and the jewels she'd converted to cold, hard cash had won her acceptance by the Dakota's exclusive enclave that over the years had included such luminaries as Judy Garland, Rudolph Nureyev, Leonard Bernstein, Bono and John Lennon, who was tragically murdered just steps from the front entrance.

Zia knew the duchess had almost been forced to sell her apartment not long ago. The apartment and her determination to educate her granddaughters in the manner she insisted was commensurate with their heritage had drained her resources. Bad investments by her financial advisor had sucked away most of the rest.

When Sarah married her handsome billionaire, she'd known better than to offer to pay her grandmother's living expenses. The duchess's pride would never allow it. But Charlotte *had* allowed Dev to sink what little remained of her savings in several of his wildly successful business ventures. And Gina's husband, Jack, had added to the duchess's financial security with investments in blue-chip stocks. Charlotte could now live in splendid luxury for the rest of her life.

This development pleased the uniformed doorman who made his stately way to help Zia from the taxi almost as much as it did the St. Sebastians. Sarah and Gina considered Jerome one of the family. He'd treated them to candy and ice cream during their schoolgirl years, scrutinized their high school dates with steely eyes, attended their weddings and delighted in the lively twins.

He'd taken Zia under his wing, too, when Charlotte had invited her to live at the Dakota. As kind as he was dignified, Jerome had acquainted the new arrival with such intricacies as subway schedules, jogging paths and the best pastrami this side of Romania. Which is why Zia made sure she paid the cab fare even before the driver pulled up at the curb. There was no way she would keep Jerome standing in the icy wind.

"Welcome home, Doctor."

He would no more think of dropping her title than he would Lady Sarah's or Lady Eugenia's. But his smile was warm and welcoming as he held the door and ushered her into what was once the *porte cochère*.

"How was your Christmas?"

"Wonderful."

"And the duchess? Maria? They're enjoying being out of this ice and snow?"

"Very much so, although I suspect they'll be happy to come home after another two weeks of sun and sand."

"I suspect so, too. And if I may be so bold," he added as he escorted her to the bank of elevators, "may I say it's good to see you smiling again."

"Was I so glum before?" Zia asked, startled.

"Not glum. Just tired. And," he said gently, "somewhat troubled."

Jézus, Mária és József! Was she so transparent? Surely she did a better job of sublimating her inner self when working with patients.

"You hid it well," the doorman hastened to assure her. "But a keen eye and an ability to assess character comes with this job." He paused, searching her face. "Did you find the solution to whatever was distressing you in Texas?"

She had to hide a smile at the slight but unmistakable

emphasis on the last word. New York born and bred, Jerome would find it hard to believe the answer to anyone's problems couldn't be found right here in the city. And to tell the truth, Zia wasn't quite sure how those stolen hours with Mike had lifted some of the weight of the decision that still hung over her like an executioner's ax, but they had. They most definitely had.

"Not the solution, perhaps," she said as the elevator door pinged open, "but a very potent antidote."

Propping the door with one hand, she took her bag in the other and leaned in to kiss the doorman's cheek.

"Just so you know," she added, "the antidote plans to make a trip to New York in the next week or so. His name's Brennan. Michael Brennan."

"I'll be sure to ring the apartment the moment Mr. Brennan arrives," Jerome replied with a twinkle in his eyes.

Strange, Zia thought as she keyed the front door and let herself into the black-and-white-tiled foyer. She still faced a wrenching decision. Yet now opting for research instead of hands-on medicine didn't feel like such a traitorous act. The possibility of a substantial grant from GSI to underwrite that research had given it impetus. She could be part of a team that pinpointed sources of deadly infections. Reduced risks to hospital patients. Saved lives.

First, though, she had to draft the proposal Rafe Montoya had outlined. She'd get on the computer, she decided as she dropped her bag in her bedroom and went to the bathroom. Right after she'd soaked long enough to ease her aching hip and thigh and calf muscles. Mike Brennan, she acknowledged with a rueful grin, had given her a lesson in anatomy unlike any she'd taken in med school.

She was at the hospital early the next morning. Those residents who'd worked through Christmas greeted her return with relief.

"Hope you're rested and ready to go," Don Carter warned. Happily married and totally stressed, he couldn't wait to shed his stethoscope for a long-anticipated New Year ski trip to Vermont. "We've been slammed with the usual spike in heart attacks and acute respiratory failures."

Zia nodded. Contrary to the popular misperception that the sharp increase in holiday deaths was driven by substance abuse, family-related homicides or depression-driven suicides, she now knew other significant causes came into play. A major contributing factor was that people who felt ill simply put off a trip to the hospital, choosing instead to be with their families over Christmas or New Year's.

Holiday staffing was also an issue, especially at Level 1 trauma centers, where seconds could mean the difference between life and death. Recognizing that fact, Mount Sinai's various centers, schools and hospitals paid careful attention to staff levels during this critical period.

Even with the controlled staffing, however, the holidays kept everyone hopping. Zia quickly fell back into the hectic schedule of morning team meetings, patient exams, family-centered rounds, chart reviews, one-on-ones with her interns and day-end team sessions. She still had two weeks in the Pediatric Intensive Care Unit before she completed that rotation. And, as they always did, these desperately ill kids tugged at her heart. Some cried, some screamed, but others showed no reaction to the catheters and IVs and high-dosage drugs that made them groggy or nauseous or both.

This was particularly true of the five-month-old admitted the second day after Zia's return. The infant lay listless and unmoving, his skin sallow and his eyes dull. She said nothing while one of her interns read aloud the admitting physician's chart notations. Nor did she offer an opinion or advice while he examined the patient under his parents' worried eyes.

When her small group had adjourned to the hall outside the nursery however, she quizzed the intern. "Did you note any anomaly in Benjamin's penis?"

She always referred to her patients by first name to insure neither she nor her students ever forgot they were treating living, breathing humans.

"I…uh…" The intern looked from her to his fellow students and back again. "No."

"It appeared elongated to me. Combined with his low birth weight and failure to thrive, what does that suggest to you?"

The intern bit his lip and searched his memory. "Low-renin hypertension?"

The genetic defect was rare and difficult to diagnose. She didn't blame the intern for missing it on the first go-around.

"That's what it looks like to me. I would suggest you have the lab measure his renin level and compare it to his aldosterone."

"Will do."

"If the ratio's too low, as I suspect it may be, let's get a consult from the Adrenal Steroid Disorders group before we discuss his condition with his parents."

Relief and respect reverberated in the fervent reply. "I'll take care of it."

Jézus! Had she ever been that young? Ever that terrified of doing more harm than good?

Of course she had.

That thought stayed with her as she crossed the catwalk connecting the Kravis Children's Hospital with the tower housing the school of medicine's research center. As head of the world-renowned facility, Dr. Wilbanks and his staff occupied a suite of offices with a bird's-eye view of Central

Park. Zia confirmed her appointment with the receptionist, then stood at the windows to admire the landscape. From this height, the frozen reservoir, rolling fields and bare-branched trees were a symphony in gray and icy white.

The buzz of the intercom brought her around. The receptionist listened for a moment and nodded to Zia. "Dr. Wilbanks will see you now."

Roger Wilbanks's physical stature matched his reputation in the world of pediatric research. Tall, snowy haired and lean almost to the point of emaciation, he greeted Zia with a burning intensity that both flattered and intimidated.

"I hope you've come to tell me you've decided to join our team, Dr. St. Sebastian."

"Yes, sir, I have."

As soon as the words were out, a thousand-pound boulder seemed to roll off Zia's shoulders. This was right for her. She'd known it somewhere deep inside for months but hadn't been able to shake the feeling that she would be abandoning the youngest, most helpless patients.

That guilty sense of desertion, of turning her back on her young patients, was gone. Part of that was due to Dr. Wilbanks's validation of her initial research. And part, she realized, was due to Mike Brennan. He'd triggered an interest in a world outside of pediatric medicine. She was light-years from expanding her research to the wider population of ships' crews and prison populations, but Mike had opened whole new vistas that gave the sterile environment of a lab new, exciting dimensions.

The possibility GSI might contribute to her research sparked an interest on the part of Dr. Wilbanks, as well. "Global Shipping Incorporated?" he echoed, his brows soaring above his rimless half-glasses. "They suggested they might fund a study of hospital-acquired infections in newborn infants?"

"They're interested in any research that might pinpoint

sources of infection. Apparently MRSA is as much a worry in the maritime world as it is in hospitals."

His brows remained at full mast while Zia walked him through the paper copies of the slides Rafe Montoya had printed out for her. The chart listing the studies GSI had funded or contributed to proved especially riveting. By the time she finished, she could almost see the dollar signs gleaming in her mentor's eyes.

"When do you present your current study to the faculty?" he asked.

"The second week in January. I don't have a specific day or time yet, but…"

"I'll take care of that. In the meantime, you need to get to work on a proposal for an expanded study. I'll have one of the senior research assistants work with you on that. You also need to talk to someone in the comptroller's office. Unfortunately, requesting and acquiring grants has become a complex process. So complex we often use the services of consultants. The comptroller will help you there. In the meantime, you can count your work with us as an elective and complete your residency on schedule."

He pushed away from his desk and came around to lay a collegial hand on her shoulder.

"I don't need to tell you research is the heart and soul of medicine, Dr. St. Sebastian. The public may hail Albert Sabin and Jonas Salk as the heroes who conquered polio, but neither of those preeminent scientists could have developed their vaccines without the work done by John Enders at Boston's Children's Hospital. God willing, our research into the molecular genetics of heart disease, the pathogenesis of influenza and herpes and, yes, the increasing incidence of MRSA among newborns, will yield the same profound results."

Zia couldn't have asked for a more motivational speech. Or a more ringing endorsement of her shift to full-time research. Buoyed by the increasing certainty she'd made the right decision, she traded hours with another resident so she could have dinner with Natalie and Dom the evening they flew in from Texas.

They'd come back a week before the duchess and Maria were scheduled to return. The New Year celebrations were over, the slush had morphed to grime, and the city shivered under an Arctic blast. Hunched against the cold, Zia took a cab to their apartment in the venerable old 30 Beekman Place building. It was less than a block from UN Headquarters, where Dom was still trying to adjust to his mission as cultural attaché.

The tenth-floor condo boasted plenty of room for entertainment and a million-dollar view of the Manhattan skyline. More important, as far as Natalie was concerned, it was only steps from a dog run, where she and the liver-and-white-spotted Magyar Agár exercised twice a day.

Natalie and the hound were just returning from their evening constitutional when Zia climbed out of the cab. The whipcord-lean hound greeted her ecstatically, Natalie with a hug and a smile.

"I was so surprised and excited when you called and told us you were switching to pediatric research," her sister-in-law said. "I hope you get as much fulfillment from your field as I do from mine."

"I hope so, too." She had to ask. "How did Dom react to the news that I won't be practicing hands-on medicine?"

"Oh, Zia! Your brother wants whatever you want." Her brown eyes brimmed with laughter. "You could dance naked down Broadway and Dom would flatten anyone who so much as glanced sideways at you. And speaking of dancing naked…"

She hit the elevator button and spun in a slow circle to unwind the leash wrapped around her calves.

"Mike Brennan stopped by the resort before we left."

"Why?"

"He *said* he wanted to talk to Dev about a fleet of new cargo ships his company is thinking about acquiring. But he and Dom spent quite a bit of time out on the balcony, one-on-one."

This was news to Zia. She and Mike had iMessaged each other a few times. Like most texts, they were short and only hinted at the activities cut off by her departure from Houston. Yet they also managed to convey an unsaid but unmistakable desire to pick up where they'd left off. None of Mike's iMessages had mentioned a one-on-one with her brother, however.

"How did they get along? Was any blood spilled? Bodily harm inflicted?"

"Let's just say your brother isn't making any more 'Cossack-y, I'll carve out his liver with a saber' noises."

Zia had to smile. Dom talked a good game. She couldn't count the number of dates she'd had to bring by the house so he could scope them out. Or the friends he'd subjected to intense and, to them, nerve-racking scrutiny. Yet he'd always respected Zia's intelligence and, more important, her common sense. He'd never interfered or second-guessed her choices. Not an easy task for the older brother who'd raised her from her early teens.

"By the way," Natalie said casually as the elevator arrived and the hound dragged her inside, "we expect you to bring Mike to dinner when he's in New York for that conference he's suddenly decided to attend."

"How did you…?" Laughing, Zia followed her sister and the hound into the elevator. "Never mind."

The two women exchanged a wry smile. Dominic St. Sebastian might have put his days as an undercover agent behind him. He kept a hand in the business, however. Or at least a finger.

* * *

Zia didn't exactly count the days until Mike showed up in New York. She was too busy with rounds and teaching and preparing the presentation of her MRSA study to the faculty and her fellow residents. In between, she snatched what time she could to work on the proposal for the expanded study.

Per Dr. Wilbanks's instructions, she used National Institutes of Health guidelines to draft the proposal. The first step was to describe the greatly expanded research project and what it was intended to accomplish. After that she interviewed prospective team members, detailed their credentials and ran her choices by Dr. Wilbanks for approval. Once she had the team lined up, she used their collective expertise to refine the objectives and nail down the resources required. They also put together a projected budget for the estimated life of the study. The "one million, two hundred thousand" bottom line made Zia gulp.

It caused the school's assistant comptroller to suck a little air, too. A busy, fussy type with salt-and-pepper hair and a string of framed degrees on her office wall, the financial guru felt compelled to deliver a lecture about the acquisition and disbursement of grant monies.

"I'm sure you understand that we have to be very careful, Dr. St. Sebastian. Especially with a grant in the amount you're requesting. We have an excellent record here at Mount Sinai, I'm very happy to say. But recent audits by the National Institutes of Health have uncovered waste and, in some cases, outright fraud at other institutes."

"That's why I'm here, Ms. Horton. I want to be sure we do everything by the book."

"Good, good." She glanced over the figures in the proposed budget again. "I doubt you'll pull in half of what you're requesting."

She hesitated, her lips pursed.

"We use the services of two excellent consulting firms that specialize in searching out and securing grant monies. I'll give you the contact information for both, but in this tight economy…"

She shook her head discouragingly. Zia debated whether to tell her about the GSI connection. She decided to wait until the expanded study had been approved and the hunt for funding actually got under way.

A few clicks of the assistant comptroller's keyboard produced a printed list of "grant consultants." Zia tucked it in the black Prada messenger bag Gina and Jack had given her for Christmas. It was exactly the right size to carry her iPad mini, her phone and all the paraphernalia she needed for work.

The dollars were still on her mind when she emerged from the subway at 72nd and Broadway just after seven o'clock. The Arctic cold front had finally blown itself out, but the air was still frosty enough for her to keep her head down and her shoulders hunched as she hurried the two blocks to the Dakota.

Jerome had gone off duty at six. The new night doorman, whose name Zia had to struggle to recall, intercepted her on the way to the elevators. "Excuse me, Doctor. A courier delivered this for you a short time ago."

With a word of thanks, she examined the plain white envelope he handed her. The outside contained only her name. The inside, Zia discovered with a delighted grin, contained an IOU for one carriage ride through Central Park, redeemable tonight or anytime tomorrow. Her pulse skipping, she dialed Mike's number.

"When did you get in?"

"A couple of hours ago."

"Why didn't you call me?"

"I knew you were working. So what's the deal? Are you up for a carriage ride?"

"It's freezing out there!"

"I'll keep you warm."

The husky promise sent a shiver of delight dancing down Zia's spine. She tried to remember if she'd seen any carriages during her dash from the subway. The new mayor had vowed to ban them, citing traffic safety and animal protection issues. She didn't think the ban had gone into effect but didn't remember noticing any carriages on the street.

"Why don't we decide what we'll do when you get here?"

"Fine by me. I'll grab a cab. See you shortly."

"Wait! How shortly?"

Too late. He'd already disconnected. She headed for the elevator again and keyed the door of the duchess's apartment with a fervent prayer she had time for a shower and to do something with her hair.

She didn't. The intercom buzzed while she was soaping herself down. She almost missed it over the drum of the water. Would have if she hadn't kept an ear tuned for it.

"Damn!"

She grabbed a towel but left a trail of wet footprints as she dripped her way from the bathroom to the hall intercom. "If that's Mr. Brennan, send him up."

"Yes, ma'am."

Back in the bedroom she yanked her closet doors. She was reaching for the comfortable sweats she spent most evenings in but stopped with her hand in midair. When she answered the front door a few moments later, she was wearing only the towel and a smile.

He, on the other hand, was wearing leather gloves, a charcoal cashmere overcoat and his black Stetson. Tipping the brim back with two fingers, he gave a low whistle.

"If this is how you New York City gals answer the door," he drawled as his gaze made a slow, approving circuit from her neck to her knees and back again, "I'll have to make a few more executive board meetings."

"I'm only a temporary resident," she reminded him.

"So this is a Hungarian custom?"

"Actually, it is. Public baths have been popular in my country for several thousand years. The Romans loved to luxuriate in the bubbling hot springs in and around Budapest."

"That so?" He waggled his brows in an exaggerated leer. "You have to hand it to those Romans."

Laughing, she backed into the foyer. "Are you going to just stand there and gawk or do you want to come in?"

"I not sure I can move. I'm a little weak at the knees."

"Mike, for heaven's sake! I'm getting goose bumps in places no woman should. Come in."

Seven

For the next forty minutes the towel proved superfluous. So did Mike's overcoat, suit, shirt and tie.

He'd intended to display a little couth this time. Show Zia his smooth, sophisticated side as opposed to the barefoot beach bum and everyone's favorite uncle. The two of them had been so pressed for time in Galveston, so surrounded by their loving but in-the-way families. Despite having stolen her away for two memorable nights, he hadn't had time to show her that he could be as comfortable in her world as he was in his own.

Time wasn't the only issue that had factored into his decision to go for more suave and less hot and hungry. As every one of his sisters had tried to hammer home to their brothers and spouses, women need romance. Wooing. Candles and flowers and, yes, heart-shaped boxes of chocolates.

Mike had considered various strategies to up the romance quotient on the flight from Houston. New York offered all kinds of possibilities. A carriage ride in the park, an elegant dinner for two at the latest in spot, a Broadway show. He'd even been prepared to man up and take her to a concert or opera if she'd preferred.

Then she had to open the door and drain every drop of

blood from his head. He'd damned near had a coronary right there in the hall. The hour that followed would remain etched in Mike's mind for the next hundred years.

Now they were lazing side by side on a sofa angled to catch the heat of a roaring fire, both of them more or less fully clothed. She was in warm, well-washed sweats and fuzzy slippers. He'd pulled on his shirt, pants and shoes. He liked the way her head rested on the arm he'd stretched across the back of the sofa. Was glad, too, that they'd decided to order Chinese instead of going out in the cold. Empty cartons littered the coffee table and surrounded a half-consumed bottle of California cabernet.

Mike played with a strand of her hair and let his appreciative gaze roam the elegant room. The duchess's salon, as Zia had termed it, featured parquet floors, antiques and a ceiling so high it was lost in the shadows. Flames danced in a fireplace fronted with black marble, and a tiny Bose Bluetooth speaker filled the room with the haunting strains of a rhapsody. Liszt's "Hungarian Rhapsody No. 5," Zia had informed Mike. One of nineteen he'd composed based on folk music and Gypsy themes.

"This is nice," he announced, wrapping a finger around the silky strand of hair. "Much better than a carriage ride. We'll have to go that route next time I'm in New York, though."

She tipped her face to his. The firelight added a rosy glow to her cheeks but didn't do anything for the shadows under her eyes. Mike found himself wishing he could banish them by keeping her in bed for the next week or month or decade.

"Is this a horse fetish," she wanted to know, "or just a Texas thing?"

"Neither. My secretary pulled up a list of the ten most romantic things to do in New York."

"You're kidding."

"Nope. A carriage ride through Central Park was near the top of the list."

"Not in January!"

The laugh accompanying the protest was easy, natural. But when she tugged her hair free of his loose hold and sat up to retrieve her wineglass, he could feel the subtle withdrawal.

Well, hell! He'd overplayed his hand. The doc had let it be known back in Galveston she didn't want to get in too deep, too fast. Yet he'd just pretty well let drop that *he* was already in up to his neck.

With deliberate nonchalance, he redirected the conversation. "How's the proposal coming?"

The ploy worked. Groaning, she dropped back against the sofa.

"I had no idea getting a major research project approved was such a complicated process. I'm on the third draft of the proposal now and have yet to finalize the lab protocols. And I still have to meet with one of the consultants the hospital recommended. Evidently there's a whole subspecialty of 'grant professionals' out there who make their living seeking out and securing funding for studies like this."

Mike nodded. "We've worked with a few of them."

"I'm going to make an appointment tomorrow. If nothing else, they can give me a reality check on the dollar figures."

"Want me to take a look at them?"

"Would you?" She hesitated and bit her lip. "Or would that be a conflict of interest? If we come to GSI for funding, I mean."

He flashed her a grin. "Not unless you intend to skew your study to show that GSI operates the cleanest, most bacteria-free ships at sea."

"Not hardly." She laughed again, once more relaxed. "I don't even know how I got interested in the incidence of

MRSA aboard ships in the first place. Wait! Yes, I do! You and Rafe reeled me with all those statistics."

Some women were wowed by money, Mike thought wryly. Others by extravagant romantic gestures. The way to Anastazia St. Sebastian's heart, apparently, was through a germ.

"Get your draft and let me take a look."

She pushed off the sofa and retreated down a tiled hall. When she returned, she flipped on the overhead lights, killed the music and deposited a thick file secured by a paper clip on the coffee table.

"I'm assuming you're not interested in the list of publications or bibliography."

"You assume right. Let me see the description of facilities and resources, then we'll take a look at the budget."

Nodding, she slid off the paper clip. "The research center at Mount Sinai is state-of-the-art. We'll use the computers there to collect and analyze data. Also to test samples."

"Good."

"Here's the estimate of start-up costs and first-year operating budget, broken out by personnel, equipment and overhead. The second and third pages project the costs out for an additional two years, assuming the initial results warrant continuation."

As Mike skimmed the neat columns, her commentary took on a hint of nervousness.

"I ran the figures by the hospital's assistant comptroller. She sucked some serious air when she saw the bottom line. That's when she suggested I talk to a grant professional."

"I'm not surprised. One-point-two million isn't exactly chump change in today's environment." He flipped to the next page, studied the numbers, returned to the summary. "You may want to take another look at your ratio of direct to indirect costs in year two. You show a shift to more field sampling at that point, so your direct costs will increase more than you project here."

Frowning, she leaned in for another look. "Damn! You're right. I've worked these numbers until I was cross-eyed. How did I miss that?"

"Because you worked the numbers until you were cross-eyed."

"Yet you caught it on the first pass."

"Unfortunately, I spend most of my time these days looking at numbers and not nearly enough with salt spray in my face."

He lazed back against the sofa, enjoying the way the firelight shimmered against the glossy black of her hair.

"Which brings me to another item on the top-ten list. Not as romantic as a carriage ride in Central Park maybe, but a lot more exciting."

"Mmm." The deep crease between her brows told him she was still crunching her numbers. "What's that?"

"Next month's Frostbite Regatta, hosted by the New York Yacht Club. A friend of mine is a member. He and his wife have been inviting me... Correction. They've been *daring* me to come up and help crew for years. I'll tell them I will if I can bring along a third mate."

He had her full attention now. Incredulous, she glanced from him to the draped windows and back again.

"Let me get this straight. You're inviting me to go sailing? On the open sea? In *February*?"

"Actually, we'd be sailing Long Island Sound, not the open sea but..." He rubbed his chin and appeared to give the matter some thought. "I can see how that might not appeal as much as the midwinter races in Kauai. I'd rather do those, too, if you can get away for a week."

"Kauai, like in Hawaii? Oh, Mike! You know I can't. I've got too much going on right now."

"Yeah, I figured that was out. But circle Saturday, Feb-

ruary thirteenth, on your calendar. That's the date of the
Frostbite Regatta. And as an added incentive, everyone who
survives the regatta will rig themselves out in long gowns
or tuxes for the big Valentine bash at the 44th Street Clubhouse that evening."

She was getting that cautious look again. Pulling back.
He could feel her retreating into herself. Away from him.

"I don't know my February schedule yet."

"No problem. Just give me a call when you do and we'll
plan accordingly." He kept it easy, casual, and made a show
of looking at his watch. "I'd better head back to the hotel."

"But you…" She stopped, restarted more slowly. "You
could stay here."

"I've got two fat notebooks to review before the board
meeting tomorrow morning. Besides…" He brushed a fingertip under the sooty-black lower lashes of her left eye.
"You look whipped. Get some sleep, and I'll see you tomorrow evening. We'll go out for dinner, this time."

He shrugged into his suit jacket and pulled on his overcoat before issuing a final word of warning. "Just don't
answer the door in a towel again. My system can't take
another shock like that."

Zia flipped the locks behind him and shuffled slowly
back down the tiled hall. She wasn't sure her system could
take another shock like the one that had hit her when she'd
opened the door, either.

The jolt of delight had come fast and cut deep. She
shouldn't have ignored that warning. Shouldn't have engaged in the silly exchange about the Romans and laughed
at his admission of going all weak at the knees. And she
most definitely shouldn't have enticed him into bed again.
Not that he'd required much enticing.

She wandered back into the salon and gathered the empty
cartons to carry to the kitchen. The possibility she'd wor-

ried about in Galveston was now looking all too probable. She'd thought then she could fall in love with Mike Brennan. She knew now it was more than a mere possibility.

The old hurt, the one buried deep in her heart, sent out a familiar stab of pain. Dropping the cartons in the trash, Zia flattened both hands on the kitchen counter and fought back.

Why *not* take the tumble, dammit? Why *not* let herself start imagining a future that included Mike? He knew she couldn't have children. She'd shared that agonizing reality with him their first night together. She still couldn't quite believe she'd opened up to a stranger the way she had but even then, when they'd only known each other for a few hours, he'd called to something inside Zia. His humor, the intelligence behind his easy smile, his obvious affection for his nephew and Davy's for him...

Her raging inner debate stopped dead. As her flattened palms curled into fists, all she could hear was an echo of his sister's bitter revelation. Mike's ex-wife refused to give him children...and had broken his heart in the process.

"A francba!"

Thumping the counter with her fists, she whirled and stalked out of the kitchen.

She woke the next morning prey to the same wildly conflicting emotions. She wanted to have dinner with Mike that evening. She even wanted to be crazy stupid and go sailing with him in the dead of winter, then feel his hands and his mouth and his body covering hers in the coming weeks and months. Years!

Yet wanting wasn't enough. Was it?

What about Mike? His needs, his desires? Did she have the right, the incredible selfishness, to tie his future to her past?

She was still torn between waiting and wanting when

she hit the hospital. As always, she sublimated her personal life to the hectic routine. Team meetings, patient exams and family-centered rounds consumed most of her morning, but she used a late lunch break to review the list of consulting firms the assistant comptroller had given her yesterday. As much as she hated to divert any of her project's potential funding to consultants, their success rates in securing that funding overcame her initial reluctance.

The head of the first firm she contacted was out of town until the following week. His office manager offered to set up an appointment with an assistant but given the amount of money involved, Zia opted to wait for the main man.

She tried the second firm, Danville and Associates, and was put through to the boss himself. As brief as their conversation was, Zia's description of her proposal fired Thomas Danville's interest.

"Sounds like you've done a lot of preliminary work, Dr. St. Sebastian." He spoke fast, his words staccato and filled with energy. "But one of the key services we provide is a thorough scrub before a draft proposal goes final. We're very skilled at nuancing research projects to make them more salable to private foundations and corporations."

Judging by the successes posted on their website, Zia could believe it. But given the interest Mike and Rafe Montoya had already expressed, did her proposal need nuancing?

Danville sensed her hesitation and jumped on it. "You have some reservations about working with a consultant, right? Understandable. Look, why don't we get together and I'll explain exactly what we can do for you?"

"It'll have to be soon. I want to get this in the works."

"Not a problem. In fact...I'm having dinner with another client at La Maison tonight. It's just a few blocks from the hospital. I could swing by and meet with you beforehand.

Or, better yet, you could join us for dinner. Get a firsthand testimonial from a satisfied customer."

"I'm sorry, I have other plans for dinner tonight."

"Drinks, then. It'll be easier to talk at the restaurant than at the hospital."

That was true enough. Her beeper never seemed to stop going off here at work.

"What time do you finish your shift?" Danville asked.

He was certainly persistent. Probably not a bad trait for a grant professional.

"I should be done by seven."

"Perfect. That'll give us an hour before my other client arrives. I'll see you then."

Feeling as though she'd just been swept along on a high-energy tide, Zia tried to reach Mike. She guessed he was still in his board meeting and sure enough, her call went to voice mail.

"About dinner tonight. I'm getting together with a grant consultant at seven o'clock at La Maison on East 96th. He's hooking up with another client at eight, so you could meet me then and we'll go from there."

Mike wasn't in the best of moods when the Maritime Trades Association executive board meeting finally adjourned.

The US Coast Guard had presented an excellent update on their new electronic credentialing program. Mike and most other ship owners hailed it as a welcome advance, one that would allow the crews manning their ships to apply for recertification via any computer in any country in the world.

Unfortunately, someone had gotten to the reps from the Seafarers International Union. Citing growing concerns over government surveillance of electronic communications, they'd dug in their heels. They wanted a detailed account of built-in safeguards to protect personal, medical and psychological information. Not an unreasonable demand but the resulting exchange was as exhaustive as it was acerbic. As if any system could guarantee 100 percent protection, Mike thought grimly as he retrieved his voice mails.

When he spotted Zia's name and number in his recent calls list, his gut tightened. She wanted to cancel dinner. He would bet money on it. The woman was so wary, so cautious. So damned worried about this baby thing. As if his interest in her depended on her reproductive abilities!

Thinking he might have to step up his campaign to convince her otherwise, Mike hit Play. His gut unkinked as he listened to her invitation to meet her at La Maison. He checked his watch and saw he had just enough time to go back to his hotel to shower. Better scrape off his five-o'clock shadow, too, he thought, scrubbing a palm over his chin. What he had planned for Dr. St. Sebastian tonight involved some very sensitive patches of skin.

Mike had been in business long enough to know as many deals were cut over drinks or dinner as they were in boardrooms. He hadn't thought twice about Zia meeting this consultant at what turned out to be a very small, very elegant restaurant on the Upper East Side…right up until he walked into the dimly lit bar and he spotted the slick New Yorker in the thousand-dollar suit crowding her space. Ignoring the fact that his own suit and tie had been hand tailored in Italy, Mike started toward them.

The consultant caught sight of him first. In one narrow-eyed glance he assessed the newcomer's style, size and attitude. As a result, he didn't need either Zia's warm greeting or the quick, proprietorial kiss Mike dropped on her lips to understand he was skirting dangerously close to territorial waters. He acknowledged as much with a cool smile when he stood to shake hands.

"Good to meet you, Brennan. We were just talking about you."

"That right?"

"Zia…Dr. St. Sebastian…says your corporation is a source of funding for her research project."

"A *potential* source," she corrected, shooting Mike an apologetic glance. "Actually, I was relating some of the statistics you and Rafe shared about the rate of MRSA incidents among ships' crews."

"A correlation worth exploring," Danville said smoothly.

Too smoothly. Mike concealed his instinctive dislike behind a polite nod.

"I agree. I've reviewed Dr. St. Sebastian's draft proposal, but my VP for Support Systems will have to do an in-depth analysis of the final before he brings a recommendation for funding before our board."

"Of course."

Zia picked up on the chill in the air. Her brows rose, but her smile stayed in place as she rose and hooked her coat off the back of her chair.

"I appreciate you squeezing in time to meet with me, Tom. I'll email the draft proposal to you tomorrow."

"I'll look for it."

Yeah, Mike just bet he would. He didn't comment, though, until he had Zia in a cab and she turned to him with an exasperated look.

"What was that all about?"

"I didn't like the guy."

"Obviously. Care to tell me why?"

"He was too smooth. And he was poaching. Or trying to."

"Poaching? What on earth do you…? Oh."

"Yeah. Oh."

Her mouth opened. Closed. Opened again. "Please tell me you're not serious."

The irritation he'd clamped down on in the restaurant gathered a whole new head of steam. Dammit all to hell! He backed off every time Zia turned all wary and skittish. Folded himself almost in half trying not to push her into something she wasn't ready for. There was only so much a man could take, however.

"Sorry, sweetheart. I'm dead serious."

"I don't believe this. I assumed… I thought…"

She broke off, shaking her head in disgust. Mike should have let it go at that point. Given them both time to cool down. Perversely, he fanned the fire.

"You thought what?"

"I thought this Texas cowboy stuff was just another layer! One of the many that make up Michael slash Mike slash Uncle Mickey."

He had to smile. "You forgot Miguel. He's in there, too. Probably the most anachronistic part of the mix."

"Anachronistic?" Ice dripped from every syllable. "Or chauvinistic?"

"They're pretty much the same thing where I come from."

"And that's supposed to make me feel better?"

"No," he replied, realizing too late that he needed to tread carefully, "it's not supposed to do anything but put you on notice."

Her chin came up. A dangerous glint lit her dark eyes. "Of?"

Mike knew it was too soon. He'd intended to give her time. Calm her doubts. Let her get used to the course he was steering. But the angry set to her jaw told him he'd just run out of windage.

"Remember the deal we made back in Galveston?"

Anger gave way to the wariness that hit him like a right cross. "I remember," she said cautiously. "Do you?"

"Every word. I said I would tell you if and when I approached the hurting stage."

He reached for her hand. She resisted but he folded it between both of his. Was that a slight tremor in her fingers or the hammer of his own pulse? He didn't know, didn't care.

"I'm there, Zia. I'm in love with you, or so close it doesn't matter."

The admission came easy and felt so right he asked himself why the hell he'd waited this long. He got his answer in the quick flare of panic in the dark eyes locked on his face.

"Mike, I…uh…"

"Relax." He forced a grin. "This isn't a race. Doesn't matter who gets where first. And," he said when the panic didn't subside, "you don't need to come up with an appropriate response right this minute. You've got a whole month to think it through."

"A whole month?"

"Okay, three weeks and some change. Until the Frostbite Regatta," he added in answer to her blank look.

"Holy Virgin!" Her expression went from blank to incredulous. "You're not really planning to participate in that insanity, are you?"

"Not unless you do. Although I have to say…" His grin widened. Curling a knuckle under her chin, he tipped her face to his. "My sisters all insist I look pretty hot in a tux."

Her disbelief melted into a reluctant laugh. "Do they?"

"Word of honor." He puffed out his chest. "Be a shame if you didn't get to see me in all my splendor."

"And I can't do that without freezing my ass off aboard a sailboat as it cuts through the icy waters of Long Island Sound?"

"Nope. That's the deal. You, me, wind and waves." His voice softened. Caressed. Challenged. "C'mon, Doc. Live dangerously."

Eight

Despite her unrelenting schedule, Zia was thrilled when the duchess and Maria finally returned from their Texas sojourn the last week in January. She'd rattled around in the empty apartment during her hours off for well over a month. The week in Galveston and Mike's brief visit had provided welcome diversions. She'd also had lunch or dinner with her brother and Natalie several times during the interval. But she was ready for the companionable presence of the duchess.

Thankfully, the vicious Arctic cold and damp that had caused Charlotte's bones to ache so badly had loosened its grip on the city. The temperature hovered at a balmy forty degrees the evening Charlotte, Maria, Gina and the twins arrived home. Jack was in Paris for some high-level diplomatic meeting, while Sarah and Dev had flown back to LA.

That left Dom and Natalie and Zia to greet the remainder of the Texas contingent when they drove in from the airport. The three St. Sebastians waited in the lobby with Jerome, who'd lingered an additional forty minutes after his shift ended to greet the travelers.

"We can't stay," Gina said as she hopped out of the limo to distribute hugs all around, including a big one for the delighted doorman. "The girls are tired and cranky. I need to get them home to bed. I'll see you this weekend, Grandmama, after you've rested and recovered."

She hopped back in and left it to the welcoming committee to escort the duchess inside. Zia noted with some concern that Charlotte leaned heavily on her cane as they crossed the lobby. So did Jerome. The doorman and Zia exchanged a speaking glance but neither wanted to spoil the homecoming by commenting on her uneven gait.

Yet after everyone else had dispersed and it was just the duchess and Zia settling in for a chat before the fire, Charlotte's first concern was for her great-niece. When Zia delivered the aperitif her aunt insisted on, the duchess's paper-thin skin of her palm stoked her cheek.

"I hoped to find the shadows under your eyes gone, Anastazia."

"It's been crazy here, Aunt Charlotte. I've been so busy."

"I can imagine." She accepted the snifter Zia handed her. "How did your presentation to the faculty go?"

"Great! Fantastic! Really, really good!"

Chuckling, the duchess hefted her glass in a salute. "Tell me."

Trying not to sound too self-congratulatory, Zia gave a quick recap of the nerve-racking session in front of the faculty and her fellow residents.

"They all found the statistics detailing the increase in Methicillin-resistant Staphylococcus aureus infections in neonatal facilities sobering."

"I should think so!"

"And no one challenged my correlation between the increasing number of MRSA incidents and staffing levels in neonatal intensive care units. Or," she added with deliberate nonchalance, "the need for more intensive study of MRSA in controlled environments similar to NIC units."

"Such as crew compartments on seagoing vessels?"

She shot the duchess an incredulous look. Charlotte chuckled and took a sip of her brandy. "Don't look so astonished. Mike Brennan paid me several visits after you left."

"He did?"

"He did. I suspect," she added drily, "he holds the mistaken impression I wield as much influence over my family as his *abuelita* does over his."

The comment struck Zia the wrong way. She couldn't believe Mike hadn't told her about these visits. Or that he might be conducting some kind of an end run by enlisting the duchess to exert her influence.

"Is that what he did? Ask you to plead his case for him?"

"Of course not. He's too intelligent for that. We discussed your research proposal…among other things."

"*What* other things?"

The abrupt demand had the duchess lifting a haughty brow. Skewered by that regal stare, Zia issued a quick apology.

"I'm sorry. It's just…Mike didn't tell me he'd spoken with you when he was here a few weeks ago."

"I'm not surprised," Charlotte returned. "Reading between the lines, I gather the time you two have spent together has been…" She paused. "Shall we say, intense."

Coming from the duchess, the delicate wording put spots of heat in Zia's cheeks. She took a few moments to regain her composure by downing a healthy gulp of *pálinka*. "I guess that's as good a description of our time together as any," she admitted.

The duchess's eyes might be clouded with age but they lingered on Zia's face with disconcerting shrewdness. "The man's in love with you, Anastazia. Or so close to the edge you could push him over with a single poke." Her voice softened, and her face folded into fine lines. "Why aren't you poking?"

"It's complicated."

"Tell me."

"I…"

"Tell me, dearest."

The quiet command broke the dam. Abandoning her chair, Zia dropped to her knees beside the duchess. The private pain she'd shared with no one but her brother—and Mike Brennan!—spilled out in quick, disjointed phrases.

"I had a hysterectomy. When I was in college. They had to do it to save my life. And now…now I can't have children."

She dropped her forehead. The words came more slowly now, more painfully.

"You saw Mike. He loves kids. He's terrific with them. He deserves someone who can give him the family he—"

"Bull!"

Zia's head jerked up. "What?"

"You heard me," the duchess retorted. "That's total and complete bull."

Her eyes snapping, she took her great-niece's chin in a firm grip.

"Listen to me, Anastazia Amalia. You're a sensitive, caring physician and a brilliant researcher. Far more important, you have a wonderful man who's in love with you. You should be grabbing at the future with greedy hands. Instead you're wallowing in self-pity. Stop it," she ordered briskly. "Now! This very instant!"

Zia reared back, or tried to. Charlotte refused to release her chin. Their eyes locked, faded blue and liquid black. One woman with a lifetime of great joy and great sorrow behind her, another just embarking on that perilous, exhilarating journey.

She was right, Zia realized with a crush of self-disgust. She'd been so worried about what she and Mike *couldn't* have that she'd refused to let herself focus on everything they *could*.

"Okay," she said on a shaky laugh. "I'm done wallowing."

"Good." The duchess didn't release her firm hold. "Now be honest with me. Do you love him?"

She couldn't deny it any longer. Not to Charlotte. Not to herself.

"Yes."

"Ahh." The quiet sigh feathered through the duchess's lips. Her cheeks creasing in a smile, she gave her great-niece's chin a little shake. "Then put the poor man out of his misery! Tell him how you feel."

"All right! I will."

The duchess released her grip but not her tenacious hold on the subject under discussion. "When?" she demanded.

Surrendering, Zia sank back on her heels. "He's flying in to New York for Valentine's weekend. He wants to take me sailing. In something called the Frostbite Regatta."

"Good heavens. That sounds perfectly dreadful."

"Exactly what I said!"

"Then again," Charlotte mused as she reached for her brandy and took a delicate sip, "I seem to recall that a sailboat rocking on a choppy sea can be rather erotic. If you're curled up in a bunk with the right person, of course."

Zia didn't share the duchess's musings with Mike when he called later that night to make sure the travelers had all returned home safely. She did, however, tell him that Charlotte had mentioned his visits.

"I enjoyed getting to know her a little better. She's a fascinating woman."

"She said pretty much the same thing about you."

"Not only fascinating, but very discerning." He let that hang for a moment before changing the subject. "So, where are you on your proposal?"

"It's signed, sealed and delivered. The research center's executive review committee meets tomorrow."

If…*when*…they gave the expanded study their stamp of approval, Danville and Associates would go out for funding. And if the financial gods were kind, the project would be up and running within weeks.

"Let me know what the committee decides," Mike said.

"I will."

"And I'll see you soon. I'm flying into New York the afternoon of the twelfth. I want to make sure we have time to suit you up for the regatta the next day."

"Right," she said slowly.

"You're not chickening out, are you?"

"What if the boat tips over? Do you know how quickly we could succumb to hypothermia?"

"Not gonna happen, Doc. It's been a while since I exercised my sea legs, but sailing's like riding a bicycle. It's easy once you learn the ropes."

"Oh, that's reassuring! You might be interested to know ERs treat more than three hundred thousand kids for bike injuries every year."

"Crap." He paused, no doubt thinking of his hyperactive nieces and nephews. "That many?"

"That many."

He mulled that over for a few moments before tossing out the one argument she couldn't counter. "I guess you'll just have to trust me to take care of you."

"I guess so. I'll see you on the twelfth."

Zia was conducting chart reviews with her interns when Dr. Wilbanks buzzed with word that the executive review committee had green-lighted her proposal.

"Congratulations," he said in his brusque way. "You're the first resident to have a study of this scope and magnitude approved. Who are you working with to secure funding?"

"Danville and Associates."

"Have we used them before?"

"They were on the list Ms. Horton gave me."

"Then I suggest you get with them as soon as possible and tell them to start the ball rolling."

"Yes, sir."

Zia made the call as soon as Dr. Wilbanks disconnected. Tom Danville added his congratulations, along with the suggestion that Zia come to his office so she could meet the others on his staff. She checked her schedule and set the appointment for three the following afternoon.

Danville and Associates occupied a suite of offices on the thirty-second floor of Olympic Tower on Fifth Avenue. Zia stepped out of the elevator into a sea of Persian carpets and gleaming mahogany. She cringed a little at the thought that the cost to maintain these expensive surroundings came from the commissions Danville and Associates made off proposals like hers. She'd included their commission in her budget but still…

A smiling receptionist confirmed her appointment and reached for her phone. "We've been expecting you, Dr. St. Sebastian. I'll let Tom know you're here."

Danville appeared a moment later. Zia wasn't intimately familiar with men's apparel, but the European in her had no trouble identifying the leather loafers and silk tie as Italian.

His eyes bright and brimming with high-voltage energy, he escorted her to his office. "I had my people scrub your proposal. They've lined up a hit list of potential funding sources. I think you'll be impressed."

He made quick work of the intros. Two men, one woman, all dressed as expensively as their boss. And all sporting very impressive credentials, Zia knew, from her study of Danville and Associates' website.

Elizabeth Hamilton-Hobbs took the lead. A trim brunette in a black Armani suit and a butterscotch silk blouse, she held a BS and a master's from the Wharton School of Business. Zia's field might be medicine, but even she knew Wharton was private, Ivy League and one of the top-ranked business schools in the US.

"My colleagues and I are very impressed with your proposed research project, Dr. St. Sebastian. You're investigating a dangerous trend impacting medical facilities, but you left room to explore other occupational areas, as well. As a result—"

"As a result," Tom Danville jumped in, scrubbing his upper lip in his eagerness, "we have the perfect in with the big shipping companies like MSC, COSCO and GSI. Also with state and federal agencies looking at the spread of infectious disease among their prison populations."

Hamilton-Hobbs waited for him to finish before continuing her presentation "We've prepared a target list of private corporations and health-oriented foundations. Now that your study's been approved, we'll get the solicitations in the works and—"

"Dr. St. Sebastian doesn't want to hear 'in the works,'" Danville huffed, scrubbing his upper lip again. "Neither do I."

Zia went cold. Stone-cold. She didn't need the quick glance the brunette exchanged with her colleagues to guess what lay behind it.

Their boss was flying high. Soaring. That wasn't his upper lip he was itching. That was the underside of his nose.

An irritated septum was one of the classic symptoms of cocaine snorting, right along with the fever-bright eyes and hyperactivity. Zia couldn't believe she'd missed the warning flags at their first meeting. She didn't miss them now, however. Danville must have cut a line right before she arrived.

Her glance shot from him to Hamilton-Hobbs. The other woman had to have seen the dawning realization and disgust in her client's expression. She held Zia's gaze with a steely one of her own.

"I'll be handling the solicitations personally, Dr. St. Sebastian. They'll go out this afternoon, and I promise I'll follow up on each one myself."

When Zia hesitated, the brunette laid her professional reputation on the line.

"Danville and Associates has one of the highest success rates in the country. I guarantee we'll secure the one-point-two million you require for your study."

Medicine, Zia had learned, was knowledge multiplied by experience compounded by instinct. So was life. She could get up, walk out and start over again with the next grant professional on the comptroller's list. Or she could trust Elizabeth Hamilton-Hobbs.

She nodded. Slowly. Not bothering to disguise her reluctance. "I want to be kept in the loop. Please copy me on each solicitation you send out and every response you receive."

Danville voiced an instant objection. "We'll send you weekly status reports. That's our standard policy. But we don't…"

His subordinate cut him off with a knife-edged smile.

"Not a problem, Dr. St. Sebastian. I'll keep you in the loop every step of the way."

Elizabeth held to her word. She cc'd Zia on every solicitation that went out and forwarded copies of every response that came in. In a remarkably short space of time, Danville and Associates secured more than eight hundred thousand dollars from three foundations and four private corporations.…including a quarter million promised by GSA over the projected two-year life of the study.

Rafe Montoya called Zia personally with the news. He caught her at work, busy preparing for the weekly discharge conference. It was one of Children's Hospital's most popular sessions. Attended by faculty and staff alike, the conference focused on patients with unusual diagnoses or diseases difficult to treat. One of Zia's patients would be discussed at this session—a five-year-old who'd presented with retinitis pigmentosa, mental retardation and obesity. She'd tested him for a dozen different possibilities before diagnosing the extremely rare Bardet-Biedl Syndrome. She was preparing to lead the discussion of his case, but took Rafe's call eagerly.

"Thought you might want to know GSI's executive board voted unanimously to help underwrite the study."

"Really? That's fantastic!"

She couldn't resist a little happy dance. The gleeful two-step set her stethoscope bobbling and her interns gaping. But when the initial thrill subsided, she had to ask.

"Just out of curiosity, how many members of GSI's executive board are related to the CEO?"

"Seven of the twelve," Rafe admitted with a chuckle. "If it makes you feel any better, though, the remaining five all have extensive backgrounds in the shipping industry. Your proposal struck a chord with them, Zia. Especially after I dropped a casual reminder of the multimillion-dollar MRSA suit brought by the crew of the *Cheryl K*."

"Thanks, Rafe. I really appreciate your support. I'll do my damnedest to make sure our research justifies GSI's investment."

"That's all we can ask. And it wasn't just me pushing this," he added. "Mike's been behind this project from the start. Okay, not just the project. He believes in you, Zia."

* * *

Rafe's ringing endorsement was still front and center in Zia's mind when Mike called to advise her of his arrival time on February twelfth. He caught her in the hospital cafeteria. She'd missed lunch and had dashed down to grab a frozen yogurt and a much-needed break. She was just dousing the creamy ice-cream substitute with chocolate sprinkles when her cell buzzed. She fished the iPhone out of the pocket of her white coat and balanced it between her shoulder and ear while signing the chit for her yogurt.

"Wheels down at five-fifteen," Mike announced as Zia carried her treat to an empty table. "I'll be at my hotel by six-thirty. Seven at the latest. Plan on dinner at eight, with several hours of uninterrupted quality time to follow. Or," he said with a husky laugh that raised shivers of anticipated delight, "quality time first and dinner to follow. Your choice, Doc."

"Wrong," she countered with a quick lick of her spoon.

"Which part?"

"The choice part. Anyone who can squeeze a quarter-of-million dollars out of his board of directors to study germs deserves first pick."

It was a joke. A lighthearted attempt to thank him for his support. Yet Zia sensed instantly the joke had fallen flat.

"Is this something we need to talk about?" he asked. "Our personal relationship vis-à-vis our professional responsibilities? I don't have a problem keeping them separate, Zia."

"Neither do I. I was just kidding, Mike. Although…"

Now that it was out there like the proverbial elephant in the room she couldn't ignore it.

"Is it really possible to separate them? Would you have endorsed my study if you didn't…if we weren't…"

"Lovers?" he supplied when she fumbled for the right word. "Friends? Acquaintances?"

"Involved."

That was greeted with a dead silence that thundered in Zia's ears, drowning out the rattle of the trays two candy stripers had just placed on the cafeteria's conveyor belt.

"Okay," Mike said after that pregnant pause. "Looks like we're going to have to sit down and have a long talk about tax credits and incentives for corporations to invest in research and development. They vary greatly at national, state and local levels."

"I know that."

"Did you also know Texas possesses four of this country's busiest deep-water ports? Galveston, Beaumont, Houston and Corpus Christi."

"No," she replied, a little put off by the lecturing tone.

"Houston is the tenth busiest port in the *world* in tonnage. So yes, GSI invests heavily in research we think may positively impact our industry and, oh, by the way, earns us almost as much in tax breaks as our original investment. Does that answer your question?"

"No," Zia snapped back, annoyed now. "I know how much GSI invests in research. Rafe briefed me on the figures in your office, yes?"

She could hear her accent thickening, feel the temper stirring behind it.

"My question was…and still is…would you have supported this particular project if you and I were not *involved*?"

"Dammit, woman, is that the best you can up with to describe where we are together?"

He still hadn't answered her question, but he now singed the airways. She gripped the phone and started to bite back. Would have, if she hadn't remembered her recent conversation with the duchess.

She owed Mike the truth. She might have given it if he hadn't just come down on her with both feet. Gritting her teeth, she forced a cool reply.

"Do you not think this is something we should discuss in person?"

"No," he shot back, as irritated now as she was. "I told you I wouldn't push you. I also remember saying this isn't a race. But I think I need some indication of whether you're even on the track."

"Jézus, Mária és József!" Goaded, she spit out the truth she'd owned up to so recently. "I love you! There! Is that what you wish to hear?"

The pause this time was longer. Moments instead of seconds.

Embarrassed by her heated outburst, Zia glanced around to see if any of the other cafeteria customers had tuned in. None had, and despite her simmering irritation she found herself holding her breath until a slow drawl came across the airwaves.

"Oh, yeah, darlin'. That's exactly what I wanted to hear. Maybe not quite in that tone, but I'm not complaining."

She could hear the laughter in his voice. And something deeper, something that locked her breath in her chest.

"Care to repeat it?" he asked, a caress in each word. "Without the attitude this time?"

How in God's name did he do this? Spark her temper one moment and make her melt the next? Sighing, Zia stabbed her spoon into the melting yogurt.

"I love you."

"There now. That wasn't so hard, was it?"

"Yes, it was! I was going to wait until this weekend to tell you, in the proper setting."

"Aboard a sailboat while we're freezing our asses off?"

"No, you fool. Before that. Or at the ball afterward."

She gave a hiccuping laugh. "I hadn't nailed down the specifics."

"Tell you what. You decide on the venue and we'll do this again in person. Deal?"

A smile spread across her heart. "Deal."

Nine

To Zia's infinite relief, she didn't get to experience the thrill of chopping through the icy waters of Long Island Sound. A front rolled in Friday afternoon, bringing with it a dense fog. Every airport on the East Coast shut just hours before Mike's private jet was scheduled to land. He had to divert to Pittsburgh and wait it out.

The impenetrable mist continued to blanket New York well into Saturday morning, forcing the yacht club to postpone their Frostbite Regatta. The Valentine Ball, however, remained on schedule for that evening. Mike promised he'd arrive by plane, train or rental car to escort her to the big bash.

The duchess took advantage of the delay to arrange a shopping expedition. Zia had already called Gina to ask if she could borrow one of her many gowns, but Charlotte dismissed that with a wave of one hand. "Nonsense. You have a very distinct style, quite different from Gina's."

"I've lived in white coats and sweats for almost three years," Zia protested. "If I had a distinctive style, it's dead and buried."

"Then we shall have to resurrect it."

Conceding defeat, Zia buzzed down and asked Jerome

to hail a taxi. It was waiting curbside when the two women emerged into the gray, drizzly afternoon a little past one o'clock.

The doorman opened the rear door with a flourish. "Where shall I tell the driver to take you, Duchess?"

"Saks Fifth Avenue."

"Of course."

The cabbie zipped through the light weekend traffic and pulled up less than thirty minutes later at the mecca for shoppers with discriminating tastes and the money to indulge them. Saks's flagship store first opened in 1924 and now covered an entire city block. Its seventh-floor café looked down on the spires of St. Patrick's Cathedral. Every floor above and below offered an array of tempting, high-end goods.

Charlotte had been forced to dispense with the services of a personal shopper during the lean years. Since Sarah married and her husband had taken over management of the family's finances, however, she was once again able to indulge in one of life's more decadent luxuries.

The ponytailed personal attendant had been alerted by a phone call from Jerome and was waiting curbside to help his clients out of the cab. "What a delight to see you again, Duchess."

"And you, Andrew."

"How may I assist you today?"

"This is my great-niece, Dr. Anastazia St. Sebastian. She requires a ball gown, shoes and an appointment at the salon."

"A pleasure to meet you, Dr. St. Sebastian." The shopper measured Zia's lithe figure and distinctive features with something approaching ecstasy. "I'm sure we can find just what you're looking for."

Mere moments later he had them ensconced in a private viewing room on the fifth floor. Crystal flutes shared a silver tray with iced champagne and bottles of sparkling water.

"May I ask if you have a particular style or color in mind?" Andrew asked as he poured champagne for Charlotte and a Perrier for Zia.

"No frills," the duchess pronounced. "Something sleek and sophisticated. In midnight blue, I think. Or..." She cocked her head, assessing Zia with the discerning eye that had once filled her closets with creations from the world's most exclusive designers. "Red. Shimmering, iridescent red."

"Oh, yes!" Andrew almost clapped his hands in delight. "With her ebony hair and dark eyes, she'll look delicious in red. Emily! Madeline!" A snap of his fingers made the two waiting saleswomen jump. "What do we have that might fit the bill?"

"It's Valentine's week," the older of the two women reminded him. "We're swimming in red."

"Well, show the duchess and Dr. St. Sebastian what we have."

The women disappeared and returned mere moments later with an array of designer originals. Each, Zia noted, was more expensive than the last. Not that she was particularly concerned about the price tag. Charlotte had flatly refused to let her contribute to household expenses for the past two and a half years. She'd insisted instead that her great-niece's company in the big, empty apartment was more than enough recompense. So Zia had banked her entire salary and could well afford to splurge on something outrageously expensive.

She tried several designs and labels, but the moment she slithered into a tube of screaming scarlet, she knew that was the one. The front bodice was cut in a straight slash from shoulder to shoulder. The back, however, plunged well below her waist. And every step, every breath, set off tiny pinpricks of light from the sparkling paillettes woven into the fabric.

Three-inch stilettos and a clutch bag in silver completed the ensemble, but the duchess wasn't done. After high tea at the seventh-floor café with its magnificent views, the two women hit the salon. They emerged three hours later. Charlotte's snowy hair was arranged in a regal upsweep. Zia wore hers caught high behind one ear with a rhinestone comb, falling in a smooth black wing over the other.

It was almost six when they returned home. Mike had called to let Zia know he'd made it into the city okay and would pick her up at seven. That left a comfortable margin to freshen up, shimmy into her gown and apply a little more makeup than her usual swipe of lip gloss. She was adding mascara to her thick lashes when the duchess tapped lightly on her bedroom door.

"Oh, my dear!" Charlotte's blue eyes misted a little as she had Zia perform a slow pirouette. "You've inherited the best of the St. Sebastian genes. There's Magyar in your eyes and high cheekbones, centuries of royal breeding in your carriage. You do the duchy of Karlenburgh proud, my dear."

Charlotte's praise stirred a glow of pride. Zia had indeed inherited a remarkable set of genes. The fierce Magyars who'd swept down from the steppes on their ponies…the French and Italian princes and princesses who'd married into the St. Sebastian family in past centuries…the Hungarian patriots who'd fought so long and so hard to throw off the Soviet yoke… They'd all contributed to the person she was. She felt the beat of their blood in her veins and a wash of surprise when the duchess pressed a small velvet box into her hand.

"These are part of your heritage, and my gift to you."

Zia flipped the lid on the box to reveal a pair of ruby

earrings nested in black velvet. Each red oval dangled from a smaller but similarly cut diamond.

"Oh, Charlotte! They're beautiful. I'll certainly wear them tonight, but I won't keep them. You should give them to one of the twins."

"I've managed to preserve a few pieces for my great-grandchildren. And Dev, clever boy that he is, has helped me reclaim some I was forced to sell over the years. These," she said with a sniff of disdain, "were apparently purchased by an extremely vulgar Latvian plutocrat for his mistress. I didn't ask Dev how he recovered them, although I understand Jack had to step in and exercise some rather questionable behind-the-scenes diplomatic maneuvering. Now," she finished firmly, "they're yours. Let's see how they look on you."

Zia thought they looked magnificent.

So did Mike when he arrived a few moments later.

When Zia met him at the door, what looked like an acre of pleated white shirtfront and black tuxedo filled her vision. He carried his overcoat over his arm, his hat in his hand and an awed expression on his face.

"Wow. You, Dr. St. Sebastian, are stunning."

"It's the earrings." She bobbed her head to set the rubies dancing. "Charlotte gave them to me, insisting they're part of my heritage."

"Trust me," he growled when she turned to precede him through the foyer, "it's not the earrings. You sure that dress won't get us both arrested?"

She was laughing when she left him to say hello to the duchess while she fetched her wrap…and thoroughly surprised for the second time that evening when she exited the lobby to find a black carriage with bright yellow wheels drawn up at the curb. The driver wore a top hat and voluminous red coat. A jaunty red plume decorated his horse's headpiece.

Zia came to a dead stop. "You've *got* to be kidding."

"Nope. I decided to do it up right this evening."

"You do know it's February, right? There's still frost on the ground."

"Not to worry. Natalie sent along a warm blanket. And your brother provided this." He fished a thin silver flask out of his pocket and held it up with a smug grin. "It's not *pálinka*, but Dom guarantees it'll warm the cockles of your heart. Whatever the hell those are," he added as he took her elbow to help her climb aboard.

"The ventricles," Zia murmured while he settled beside her. "From the Latin, *cochleae cordis*. When did you see Natalie and Dom?"

"Right before I came to pick you up." He draped the blanket over her knees and settled his hat on his head before stretching an arm across her shoulders to keep her close for added warmth. "All right, Jerry. Let's go."

The driver nodded and checked over his shoulder for traffic before clicking to his horse. Still slightly dazed to find herself clip-clopping down Central Park West, Zia felt compelled to ask.

"Did you stop by Natalie and Dom's just to pick up a blanket and brandy?"

"Pretty much. Although *abuelita* suggested it would be a smart move to let your brother know I intended to ask you to marry me. I wasn't too keen on the idea," he admitted with a grimace. "At best, Dominic considers me a half step above a freebooter. But I figured I…"

"Wait! Back up!"

"To what? Freebooter? It's an old Dutch term for pirate." He attempted to look innocent but the gleam in his eyes gave him away. "Or do you mean the part of about telling Dom I intend to propose?"

"You know very well that's what I mean!"

"Well, I have to say His Grace wasn't all that happy about his sister hooking up with a lowlife Texas wharf rat. But after some abject begging on my part and several comments from Natalie about *his* lifestyle prior to marriage, Dom conceded it was your decision."

Zia's mind whirled with images of swashbuckling pirates and Dom assuming his haughtiest grand duke demeanor and Mike trying his best to appear abject. She was still trying to sort through the kaleidoscope when he used the arm draped across her shoulders to angle her into a close embrace. His breath warmed her cheek, and his eyes smiled down into hers.

"Why look so surprised? What did you think was going to happen after you threw that bombshell at me over the phone?"

"I *thought* we were going to talk about it this weekend, at a time and venue to be decided.".

"We could talk, I suppose, but it makes more sense to me to cut right to the chase. I love you. You love me. What else matters, Anastazia Amalia Julianna St. Sebastian?"

"Did Dom make you memorize all my names?"

"No, that was Natalie. Your sister-in-law," he added with a touch of awe, "is a powerhouse packed in a very demure, very deceptive package. I'm not sure I want to get her and my sisters in the same room at the same time. The males on both sides of our respective family trees might never recover."

A thousand questions had swirled through Zia's mind. Where would they live? How would marriage affect her appointment to Dr. Wilbanks's research team? When, if ever, would she return to her homeland? But his comment about family trees pushed everything else out of her head.

"We *do* need to talk, Mike." She threw a quick glance at the driver and dropped her voice. "We're making a life decision here and I don't even know how you feel about adoption. Or fostering. Or using a surrogate or...or not having children at all."

"Look at me."

His eyes lost their teasing glint and he, too, lowered his voice to give her gut-wrenching worry the seriousness it demanded.

"I'm good with *any* of those options, Zia. As long as we make the decision together."

"But your family...your sisters..."

"This isn't about them. It's about us. You and me, spending the rest of our lives together. I want to sail the Pacific with you and show you my world. Tag along behind you at the hospital to learn more about yours. When and if we decide to bring children into the world we create together, we'll figure out the best way to do it. All that's required at this moment is a simple 'yes.'"

The old hurt, the sense of loss Zia had carried since that long-ago ski trip, was still buried deep in her psyche. She suspected it would never fully disappear. But a burgeoning joy now overlaid the ache. The duchess was right. She had to reach out and grab the future with both hands.

Literally *and* figuratively. Sloughing off her doubts, she hooked both hands in the lapels of Mike's overcoat and tugged him closer. "Yes, Michael Mickey Miguel Brennan. Yes."

When he moved in to seal the deal with a kiss, Zia knew she would always remember this snapshot in time. Whatever came, whatever the future he'd sketched for them brought, she would feel February's nip. Hear the horse's hooves clacking on the cold pavement, the carriage wheels rattling out their winter song.

Then he surprised her with another memory to tuck away and savor. This one included a jeweler's box. Her second of the night, Zia thought with a wild thump of her heart. She raised the lid, her fingers a little shaky, and gasped when the pear-shaped diamond caught the glow of the streetlamps.

"I had to guess at your ring size," he confessed as he plucked the ring out of its nest and eased it over her knuckle. "The fit looks pretty good to me, though."

Not just the fit. The size and clarity and the fact that it adorned her finger had Zia swinging between delight and disbelief. She'd met this man less than two months ago and now wore his ring. It was only a symbol. A *very* expensive token. Yet it shouted to the world she and Mike intended to make a life together. She'd never appreciated the awesome power of symbols before.

She tucked her hands under the blanket and fingered the ring throughout the ride. The raised mounting and sharp, V-shaped prong protecting the pear's pointed tip had almost drawn blood by the time they arrived at the New York Yacht Club.

Hemmed in on three sides by towering skyscrapers, the club was a bastion of old Manhattan now immortalized as a National Historic Landmark. Light poured from the huge windows fronting West 44th Street. Fashioned to resemble the elaborate transoms of Spanish galleons, the windows gave tantalizing views of an immense interior room lined with scale models of members' yachts.

Hundreds of scale models, Zia discovered after she and Mike had checked their coats and joined the glittering crowd. Thousands! Some with sails furled, some in full rigging. They were mounted on lit shelves that filled almost every inch of the fantastic room's walls, leaving space only for a monstrous white marble fireplace decorated with tridents and anchors and an oval painting of a ship in full sail. Zia rested her arm lightly in the crook of Mike's arm and craned her neck to take in all the nautical splendor.

"Mike!"

A short, sturdy fireplug of woman with iron-gray hair and leathery skin cut through the crowd. A distinguished and much taller gentleman trailed in her wake.

"That's Anne Singleton," Mike advised as the woman plowed toward them. "Her husband and I served in the navy together."

Zia appreciated the brief heads-up, especially after Anne latched on to Mike's lapels and hauled him down for a loud, smacking kiss. She broke the lip-lock but hung on to his tux.

"Can't believe we finally got you up here to the Frost-bite Regatta and the damned thing gets postponed! Promise you'll come when we reschedule."

"We'll see."

"If you're done with him, Annie, mind if I say hello?"

The mild exposition came from the man Zia assumed must be Singleton's husband. His wife relinquished her hold and used the brief interval while they shook hands to inspect Zia from head to toe. All of a sudden she let out an earsplitting whoop.

"He did it!" Her leathery face creased into a wide grin. Eyes alight, she jabbed an elbow into her husband's side. "Harry! He did it!"

"I see," he replied, wincing.

Zia didn't, until Mike explained. "After cooling my heels so long in Pittsburgh this morning, I wasn't sure I'd get here in time to pick up the ring. Tiffany's said they would courier it to my hotel, but just to be safe I called Anne and asked her to pick it up, then meet me at the airport."

"Which I was so thrilled to do! You have no idea how many women I've tried to hook this man up with in the past three years. I've run through every one of my single, divorced and widowed friends, the *daughters* of those friends, the *friends* of those…"

"I think she's got the picture, Anne."

"Oh hush, Harry! You paraded a few past him, too. Remember that bottle blonde you invited to the races in Newport? Worst weekend of my life," his wife confided with a shudder. "The woman had a laugh that could strip the paint from a steel hull."

"True," her husband conceded good-naturedly.

They were so different, Zia thought. One so tall and elegant in his tux, the other wearing what was probably a ten-thousand-dollar designer original with complete disregard for the way it hitched up on one shoulder and bunched around her sturdy hips. Yet the affection between them was obvious and heartwarming.

"I'm Harry Singleton, Dr. St. Sebastian. I don't know if Mike told you, but he and I go way back."

"Please call me Zia. And, yes, he mentioned that you served in the navy together."

"Did he also mention that he saved my ass when I went overboard in the Sea of Japan during Typhoon Ito?"

"No."

She threw Mike a questioning glance, but Anne Singleton waved an impatient hand. "You can bore her with your war stories later. Right now we need to toast this momentous occasion."

She detached Zia from Mike, caught her arm and hauled her toward a table groaning with crystal and china bearing the yacht club's distinctive insignia etched in gold. Two other couples lingered by the table, cocktails in hand. While her husband signaled to one of the hovering attendants, Anne introduced Zia to their obviously close circle of friends.

"That's Alec, former conductor of the Lincoln Center Orchestra," she said, stabbing a finger at each of the four in turn. "Judy, his wife and the lawyer you want if you're ever charged with tax evasion. Helen, mother of five and the world's greatest cook. Dan, who's yet to miss one of

Helen's meals. Okay, now listen up, crew. This is Zia St. Sebastian. She and Mike are about to hook the bight."

Zia's puzzled look generated grins all around and several equally unintelligible phrases.

"Fit double clews," Harry supplied, his eyes twinkling.

"Get spliced," the retired conductor put in.

"Also," Judy drawled, "known as getting hitched." She rounded the table and took both of Zia's hands in hers. "I know protocol says you're supposed to congratulate the man in this situation, but I think everyone at this table will agree you've won a real prize."

Zia didn't need to hear Mike's low groan to know his friends had acutely embarrassed him. She, on the other hand, was delighted to discover yet another dimension to his multifaceted personality. A side of him this group obviously cherished. A side she was suddenly, voraciously eager to explore.

The rest of the evening passed in whirl of color and music. The seven-course dinner was a gourmand's delight. The live band provided dreamy music during and after the meal. What kept Zia laughing, though, were the personal recollections that grew more incredible and less believable as the night progressed. Interestingly, there was only one mention of Mike's previous plunge into stormy matrimonial waters. It was couched in an obscure nautical term that dropped Zia's jaw when Anne whispered a translation.

Her sides were still aching when she and Mike collapsed in the backseat of a taxi well past one in the morning. By unspoken consent they went to his hotel. And, again by mutual consent, they called the duchess the next morning to ask her permission for a family gathering at the apartment later that afternoon.

Natalie and Dom showed up. So did Gina and Jack and the twins. Maria made a special trip in, and even Jerome managed to pop up for a quick glass of champagne.

After the toasts and hearty congratulations, Dom engineered a few moments alone with Zia. They stood at the windows overlooking Central Park, two foreigners with unbreakable ties to America...and Americans.

"This is what you want?" he asked softly in their native Hungarian.

"Yes."

"It's not easy to blend two worlds, two nationalities."

"You and Natalie don't seem to have had any problems."

"We haven't," Dom agreed, his gaze drifting to his wife. "But Natalie is altogether unique."

"So is Mike."

His glance came back to Zia. The love in his eyes flooded her heart. "Then I wish you all the joy that I've found, little one."

"Thank you."

An hour later, Zia kissed Mike goodbye. She hated to see him go. This separation loomed so much larger than their previous weeks apart. It also resurfaced her concerns about where they'd live and how they'd merge their very different careers.

"We'll work it out."

"Before or after we're married?"

"Whenever."

"Mike..."

Her snort of exasperation made him smile, but his eyes turned dead serious as he curled a knuckle under her chin.

"We Texicans are thickheaded as hell, darlin'. Stubborn, too. But I've been down this road before. Nothing and no one matters to me more than you do. We'll work out the minor details."

Mike made pretty much the same declaration to his family when he returned to Houston and announced his engagement. Eileen took considerably more convincing than the rest. Probably because she'd seen him at his lowest point after his divorce.

Mike hadn't been happy then, when his sister had tracked him to one of Houston's sleaziest waterfront dives. And he wasn't happy now, when she marched into his office unannounced and uninvited. It didn't faze his sister that he was on a teleconference with Korea. She planted a hip on the corner of his desk, crossed her arms and waited.

"I like Zia," she said the moment he disconnected. "I do! And I get down on my knees every night to thank God she was there to drag Davy out of the undertow. But you've known her for what? Six weeks?"

Mike set his jaw, but she ignored the warning.

"That's two weeks less than you knew The Bitch before you waltzed her to the altar."

"Eileen…"

"I don't want to see you hurt again, Mike. None of us do." Tears filmed her eyes. "Please tell me you know what you're doing."

The tears took the sting from his anger. He pushed out of his chair and came around to drape an arm across her shoulders.

"Jill was heat and hunger and lust. Zia's…" He searched for the impossible words to describe her. "Zia's what you and Bill have," he said finally. "What Kate and Maureen and our parents and *abuelita* all found. What I need."

His sister heaved a resigned sigh. "Since you put it that way…"

He thought he was home free after that. Right up until the middle of March, when Rafe came into his office just hours after Mike's return from a three-day meeting in Seoul. A frown creased his brother-in-law's forehead and his dark eyes telegraphed trouble. Still, Mike wasn't prepared for his uncharacteristically hesitant opening salvo.

"You remember the bottom line on Zia's MRSA study?"

"One point two mil and some change." A knot formed low in Mike's belly. He'd worked with Montoya long enough now to read his VP for Support System's unspoken signals. "Why?"

Rafe scowled at computer printouts in his hand and framed a slow, careful reply. "The change seems to have multiplied since the original proposal. And I'm damned if I can figure out why."

Ten

With Rafe's words hanging heavy in the air, Mike got out from behind his desk. "Let's take this to the conference table. You need to show me exactly what's got you concerned."

The table was a slab of thick glass supported by a bronze base. It seated twenty and had hosted too many high-level negotiations and contract signings for Mike to count. Those billion-dollar deals weren't on his mind as Rafe spread out his pencil-annotated reports, however. What concerned him was a specific project that GSI had helped fund to the tune of a quarter-of-a-million dollars.

"The study's direct costs track," Rafe said, spreading out a series of documents. "Zia's initial report accounts for every hour her team spent refining their objectives and setting up their base of operations. Ditto expenses for supplies and equipment, hours logged on the center's computers and fees paid to their outside funds consultant."

Mike frowned as he skimmed the fees charged by Danville and Associates. The total was on the high side, but not out of the ballpark compared to those charged by other firms that specialized in securing and managing grant monies. He just couldn't get past his instinctive and purely personal gut reaction to Danville himself.

"The discrepancy's in the indirects," Rafe was saying as he flipped several pages.

Well, hell! Mike had warned Zia to check her indirects.

They were tricky at best. A soft area encompassing overhead expenses like administrative support, utilities and depreciation for buildings and equipment. Usually the parent institution—in Zia's case Mount Sinai's school of medicine—negotiated with the United States Department of Health and Human Services every four years or so to determine its indirect cost rate. Unfortunately, those negotiations weren't based on any hard-and-fast mathematical formula. They had to take into consideration such intangibles as the school's academic standing, salary levels of their professors compared to other institutions, and so on.

"As you know," Rafe said, echoing his thoughts, "indirect rates can vary anywhere from twenty to forty percent depending on the reputation of the institution involved. And even when HHS agrees to a rate, there's still considerable flex in the process."

He flipped to another printout. This one showed the amounts contributed by private foundations and corporations.

"Not all of Zia's investors funded her indirects at the same percentage. These two didn't fund the indirects at all."

Mike zeroed in on a single entry. "But GSI did."

"Yes, we did. We also approved the formula the university uses to determine how much of the money we send them goes into their general operating fund and how much goes back to Zia's project."

Rafe paused and stroked a fingertip along his pencil-thin mustache. An unconscious habit, Mike knew. One that suggested he'd damned well better sit up and pay attention.

It also usually indicated he wouldn't like what his VP for Support Systems was going to say next.

"That redistribution doesn't happen automatically. The project manager has to request it."

"What are you telling me? Zia hasn't requested her indirects?"

"Yeah, she has. Or rather, the agency managing her project funds has."

"Danville and Associates."

"Right. But…" Rafe frowned at his penciled notes. "As best I can tell, they're using a different formula than the one we approved."

Mike bit down on a curse. Whatever the discrepancy—*if* there was one—this was Zia's project. When she signed her name on the bottom line of her proposal, she'd accepted full responsibility for how the money expended on the project was used.

"I'm sure Zia can explain the difference," he said with a shrug.

He checked his watch, saw it was almost three-thirty New York time and pulled out his cell phone. When his call went to her phone's voice mail, he left a message asking her to call him back, then tried the number she'd given him for her new work area at the research center. That call was answered by one of the other researchers working the project.

"Dr. Elliott."

After more than a month of communicating with Zia via email, FaceTime and phone—and one very eye-opening visit to the research center—Mike was now on a first-name basis with most of his fiancée's team.

"Hi, Jordan. This is Mike Brennan. I'm trying to reach Zia."

"She's still at lunch. I expected her back before now but it's a working session. Must be running longer than expected."

"Must be."

"I'll be happy to take a message. Or you could contact Danville and Associates. I'm sure Tom's secretary can tell you where he and Zia are having lunch."

Mike didn't skip a beat, but he could feel his fist tightening on his phone. "Just ask her to give me a call, would you?"

"Sure thing."

"Thanks."

He cut the connection and gave Rafe a quick update. "She's having a late lunch. Why don't you leave your notes and I'll go over them with her when she calls back?"

"Sure. In the meantime, I'll keep scrubbing the numbers."

Mike pushed away from the conference table but didn't return to his desk after Rafe left. Jamming his hands in his pants pockets, he faced the windows and stared unseeing at the haze belched out by Houston's millions of vehicles and dozen or so oil refineries. ExxonMobil's Baytown facility—the world's largest—processed more than five hundred thousand barrels a day. It also contributed heavily to GSI's profit margin. Even from where he stood, Mike could see two GSI tankers negotiating the bays and bayous leading to Exxon's giant facility. Yet the sight of their distinctive green-and-white hulls barely registered on his consciousness. He was still trying to understand his gut-level reaction to hearing Zia had yet to return from an extended lunch with Tom Danville.

Hell! What was the matter with him? He wasn't some Neanderthal. A throwback to the Middle Ages, jealously guarding his property. What he was, he reminded himself, was ass over end in love with a smart, savvy professional woman. One who couldn't be more different from his ex-wife if she tried. And yet...

He still remembered Jill's reaction when he'd told her

he was filing for divorce. He'd be a long time erasing the memory of her face as it twisted into a mask of fury. Or the string of affairs she'd tossed at him in retaliation. Or her snarling admission that she'd counted the hours until he'd left on another of his endless business trips. Or her shouted obscenities when he'd walked out the door for the last time.

Mike had never told anyone about that sorry scene. Not his family. Not his friends. Maybe because he knew the debacle was as much his fault as Jill's. He *had* used his rapidly expanding business interests as an excuse to escape her endless complaints. He *had* picked up more than one subtle hint that there might be more to his wife's jaunts to Vegas than casinos and high-end malls. And he'd experienced nothing but relief when their marriage was finally over.

What he had now, with Zia, represented the opposite end of the spectrum. From the moment he'd met her on the beach at Galveston, he'd felt nothing but admiration for her dedication, her brilliance, her unshakable belief that her research might make a difference. And, yeah, the woman inside those sweats and lab coats was pretty spectacular, too.

Now her research could be in trouble. Rafe hadn't come right out and mentioned fraud or mismanagement. He didn't have to. Mike didn't believe in the old saw that money was the root of all evil, but he'd seen it corrupt too many people too often. His jaw set, he whirled and strode to the outer office.

"Clear my schedule for the rest of the week, Peggy. I'm going to New York."

"Tomorrow?"

"This afternoon—or as soon as they can get the Gulfstream turned around."

The jet would have to be serviced after the flight back from Seoul and a new crew called in. Mike would be lucky to be in the air by five, in New York by ten Eastern time. Although he wasn't jet-lagged from the Korea trip, he knew the time warp would hit with a vengeance somewhere over

Ohio. He should probably wait until tomorrow to fly but couldn't shake the need to work through this problem— whatever it was—with Zia.

Half a continent away, Zia was prey to the same itchy feeling of impatience. Against her better judgment, she'd yielded to Tom's argument they could get more done at a restaurant than at his office, where his phone rang incessantly and other clients demanded his attention. She'd also accommodated his busy schedule by agreeing to a late lunch.

His solo appearance at this cozy French bistro on Broadway and 58th had irritated her no end, however. So had his insistence that they eat before getting down to the nitty-gritty. She'd picked her way through half of her Salad Niçoise but now pushed her plate to the side and voiced her annoyance.

"I've communicated directly with Elizabeth Hamilton-Hobbs for the past month. She's my primary contact at your firm. I don't understand why she couldn't make this meeting."

"That's one of the reasons I wanted this face-to-face." Danville dabbed his mouth with his napkin and folded his expression into unhappy lines. "I know how well you and Elizabeth connected. But…well…I had to let her go."

"What! When?"

"This morning."

Zia jerked back, her shoulders slamming the padded booth. She'd worked so closely with Elizabeth these past weeks! Had come to appreciate the woman's droll sense of humor almost as much as her business acumen. When GSI approved that quarter-million-dollar grant, Zia and Elizabeth had celebrated with a bottle of Chilean Malbec. And when the rest of the funding came through, they'd treated each other to an orgy of Godiva chocolate. Now she was gone?

"What happened? Why did you let her go?"

"I really can't…" Danville paused and scrubbed a finger under his nose. "I'm sorry, Zia. I have to follow certain rules of confidentially in situations like this."

"Situations like *what*, dammit?"

"I can't say. I really can't. But I can tell you this. From now on I'll manage your funding personally."

Oh, sure! Like she was going to trust a crackhead to oversee her project's finances? She started to tell him so but pulled up short when she remembered the contract she'd signed with Danville and Associates.

How binding was it? Did she have an out? Any grounds to terminate? She'd better find out, and fast.

Grabbing her purse and hooded wool jacket, she squeezed out of the booth. "I'm not happy about this, Tom."

"Neither am I. I trusted Elizabeth."

He rose and helped her on with her coat. Zia murmured her thanks and raised her left hand to tug her hair free of the hood. The sight of her engagement ring sparked a now-familiar refrain.

"I hope your fiancé knows what a lucky bastard he is."

"I hope so, too."

He caught her hand and angled it so the pear-shaped diamond caught the light. "If any your project funding falls through," he said with a cynical twist of his lips, "you could always hock this."

She tugged her hand free and pinned him with an icy stare. "Let's hope it doesn't come to that. For *both* our sakes."

"Whoa!" He held up both palms. "Just kidding, Doc."

He'd damned well better be! Her mind churning, Zia left the restaurant and headed for the subway stop on the corner. A quick glance at her phone showed a short list of missed calls, including one from Mike. She decided to wait until she was back at the hospital to return it along with the others.

She exited the subway at Lexington and 96th and cut

over to Mount Sinai's four-block campus. Spring was still just a vague hope. Trees and bushes had yet to put out any buds and the hospital's brick-and-glass towers looked stark against the unforgiving sky.

The sounds and smells of the Children's Hospital greeted her. She'd finished her neonatal ICU rotation and now spent the majority of her time in the research center. The familiar scent of antiseptic followed her as she hurried past the labs with their gleaming equipment and ongoing experiments to the modular unit set up to house the MRSA study. The only member of the team present at the moment was Jordan Elliott, a microbiologist with a specialty in infectious diseases. Petite and vivacious, she glanced up from her computer and flashed a smile.

"Hey, Zia. How was lunch?"

"Long. Unproductive. Worrying."

"Huh?"

"Elizabeth Hamilton-Hobbs isn't with Danville and Associates anymore."

"You're kidding! When did that happen?"

"This morning, evidently. Tom wouldn't tell me why he and Elizabeth parted ways. It's some kind of confidentiality thing." Frowning, Zia shed her coat and hooked it over the back of her chair. "I need to review our contract with Danville and see what our options are."

Jordan's brows lifted but she didn't comment. This wasn't her first research study. She knew funding was a complex and multilayered process. Even more complicated with outside sources like GSI in the mix. Which reminded her...

"I almost forgot. Mike called. He wants you to call him back."

"I will," Zia promised, her gaze locked on the contract scrolling up on the computer screen.

The legalistic phrasing didn't reassure her. If she was interpreting it correctly, the only way out of the contract was if Danville and Associates failed to meet one of their stated objectives. Elizabeth had aced them all so far, not least of which was soliciting and securing every penny Zia had requested.

Only a fraction of those funds had been disbursed to date, though. Just what they'd needed to cover the start-up. Computers, furniture, subscriptions to medical and commercial databases, the first month's salaries for team members…six pages worth of direct costs. The total looked ginormous to Zia, but she knew it would climb even higher when they factored in the indirects.

With a moue of disgust, she clicked through the dizzying array of figures again before listening to her messages. The one from Mike requested a callback. He didn't answer his cell, though, so she tried his office.

"Hi, Peggy. It's Zia. I'm returning Mike's call."

"Sorry, Zia. He's already left for the airport."

"Left? I thought he just got back."

"Didn't he let you know? He's on his way to New York. They should be wheels up, um, right about now."

Surprised and delighted, Zia thanked her and tried Mike's cell again. The call went through this time, although about all she could hear was the roar of revving engines.

"I just heard you're headed this way," she shouted over the noise. "What's the occasion?"

"Do we need one?"

"I can barely hear you."

"I said… Never mind. Hang loose and I'll call you back when we're airborne."

Mike waited for the sleek ten-passenger executive jet to slice through the haze and hit open sky to make the return call. When he picked up his phone, however, the instrument buzzed in his hand and Rafe's office number popped up on the screen. He took his brother-in-law's call and had his world rocked for the second time that day.

"Have you talked to Zia?" Montoya wanted to know.

"Not yet. We've been playing telephone tag. I was just about to call her back."

"You may want to hold off on that."

The reply turned Mike's insides cold. "Why?"

"Remember I told you I was going to keep scrubbing the numbers on her indirects."

"What'd you find?"

"A disbursement code that wasn't in the original proposal. It's buried in a subset of indirects relating to utilities. But instead of linking to the university's general operating fund, the code links to a separate bank routing number."

Mike's knuckles turned white where they gripped the phone. "Bottom line this for me, bro."

"That's just it. I can't. When I tried to trace the routing number, I hit a wall. Or more precisely, a damned near impenetrable firewall."

"Oh, hell. It's a blind?"

"That's what I'm thinking."

Rafe fell silent. Mike knew there was more, though. When his brother-in-law sank his teeth into something, he didn't let go.

"You said damned near impenetrable. Did you get in?"

"No, but I did poke around enough to generate a call from a friendly FBI agent."

"Christ!"

"He's with what used to be the white-collar-crimes division, Miguel. He wanted to know why we're digging into that particular account."

"Did you tell him I'm on my way to New York? That I plan to check into this very issue myself?"

"Yeah, I did. He says he needs to talk to you first. In fact, he offered to fly up from DC tomorrow and meet you in New York. I told him I'd check with you and see if that's how you want to handle it."

Mike scrubbed a hand across his jaw. He could feel the jet lag from his trip to Seoul crawling over him now. Combined with the tension Rafe had just piled on, he felt as though he'd been hit with a pile driver.

"Mike?"

"Yeah, I'm here. Set up the meeting."

Before returning Zia's call he signaled the steward. The Gulfstream crew didn't normally include a cabin attendant on short hops within the States. Graham hadn't checked out after the transatlantic flight, however, and at this moment, Mike was happy to make use of his services.

"Would you bring me a Scotch, Gray? Neat."

"Sure thing."

The Glenlivet went down with its usual smoky fire, but the heat didn't dissipate the cold spot in Mike's stomach. Whatever way he looked at it, he couldn't see a good ending to what was smelling more and more like fraud.

Although he didn't for a second believe Zia had a hint of anything questionable in the works, she was the project manager. She'd put the proposal together. She'd signed off on the grant solicitations. She was responsible for proper distribution of funds. At the very least, a fraud investigation would hang a cloud over her project. At the worst, her reputation in the tight-knit world of pediatric research would take a hit. Not the best way to kick-start a new career.

Mike tossed back the rest of his Scotch, powered up his phone and hit the speed-dial number for Zia's cell.

"Sorry it took so long to get back to you. I had another call."

"No problem. So how was Korea?"

"Busy and productive. GSI's going to acquire six new Triple-E class super-containers over the next three years."

"Super-containers, huh? I'm getting a mental picture

of hundreds of those shipping containers piled one on top of each other."

"Try thousands. Eighteen thousand, to be exact."

"On each ship?" she asked incredulously.

"On each ship."

"Okay, I'm officially impressed." She paused before changing the subject. "I'm really glad you're flying in tonight, Mike. Something's come up. I'd like to talk to you about it."

"Personal or otherwise?"

"Otherwise."

Hell! He had to ask. "Is this related to your working lunch with Tom Danville?"

"How did you know about lunch?"

Surprise and just a hint of wariness colored the question. She obviously hadn't forgotten Mike's reaction to Danville when they'd met at La Maison.

Or was it something else?

No, dammit! He was letting this FBI business spook him! Whatever the hell was going on, there was no way Zia could be involved. Deliberately, he put a shrug in his reply.

"Jordan mentioned where you were when I called earlier."

"Oh." Another pause. "What time do you think you'll be in?"

"Late, I'm afraid. After midnight."

"You have to be dead, considering you were on the other side of the world this morning. Get some sleep tonight and I'll take off early tomorrow afternoon to welcome you home in style."

"Define style," he said with a smile, relaxing for the first time since Rafe's call.

"We could do the ballet," she teased, well aware of how he felt about it. "Or the opera. Or maybe just snuggle in with a pizza and a movie."

"Now you're talking. Your place or mine?"

"Well..." Her voice dropped to a provocative purr. "The duchess doesn't particularly care for pizza."

"This is sounding better by the moment."

She laughed and agreed. "Where are you staying this time?"

"Let me check." He pulled up the travel docs Peggy had loaded to his phone. "The W New York."

"Okay, here's the deal. I'll call you when I'm on the way with pizza. You pick the movie. But nothing X-rated," she instructed sternly. "Maybe not even R. We wouldn't want to overstimulate your poor, jet-lagged brain."

"Can't happen, kid. You walk into the room and my brain shuts down anyway. All that's left is pure, unadulterated..."

"Lust? Greed?"

"I was going to say love, but lust and greed are right there in the mix, too."

He disconnected, still smiling. Rafe's call a few minutes later wiped the smile off his face and put the kink back in his gut.

Eleven

"It's set," Mike's brother-in-law announced tersely. "Tomorrow, 9:00 a.m., at the FBI's New York office. Ask for Special Agent Dan Havers."

"Got it. Although I've got to tell you, Rafe, I don't like keeping Zia in the dark about all this."

"I understand, but…"

"But what?"

"I'm beginning to think there's more to the situation than we suspect, Miguel. I can't see a DC-based FBI agent jumping on a plane and meeting you in New York just to talk about fifty thousand in misdirected grant money."

"I've been having those same thoughts," Mike admitted grimly. "They're the only reason I didn't tell Zia about this FBI contact. The more I can find out from this guy tomorrow, the better I can help her navigate through whatever the problem is."

"Keep me in the loop, too."

"Will do."

Mike had the steward pour him another Scotch and nursed it for the rest of the flight. He nursed more than a few doubts, as well. He knew he was setting himself up for some potentially tense moments with Zia if he told her about the FBI meeting after the fact. But he also knew he was in a better position to elicit information than she was at this point. GSI was only one of several corporations contributing to the MRSA study but it had provided significant funding. Naturally Mike would want to investigate any apparent anomalies in the distribution of those funds. Especially if the person ultimately responsible for the disbursement was his fiancée.

The FBI would view Zia in a more cautious light. She was a foreign national in the United States on a work/study visa. What's more, she had close ties to some very high viz personalities. Jack Harris, Gina's husband, was the US Ambassador to the UN. And Sarah's husband, Dev, operated half the damned civilian transports in the country.

Then there was the duchess. And, Mike thought with an inner grimace, the grand duke. He didn't know much about Dominic's years as an undercover agent for Interpol. Just enough to appreciate that the FBI might be understandably wary of crossing agency lines. Looking at it from that angle made Mike feel marginally better about his 9:00 a.m. meeting.

Any delusion that the FBI was the least bit concerned about Zia's personal situation or connections shattered ten minutes after Special Agent Dan Havers met Mike in the lobby of the FBI's New York office at 26 Federal Plaza.

Havers was an athletic-looking thirty-six or -seven, with wrestler's shoulders and a tree-trunk neck that strained his white shirt and navy suit jacket. The lines etched deep around his eyes suggested white-collar crime was something other than sport, however.

"Thanks for coming in, Brennan."

Mike took the hand Havers thrust out and braced for a bone cruncher that didn't come.

"Let's get you ID'd and badged. We've got a conference room reserved. We'll talk there."

They kept small talk to a minimum until Havers ushered Mike into the twenty-third-floor conference room. Four others—two men, two women—were waiting his arrival. Three clustered around the coffee and pastries at the far end of the room. One stared moodily through the blinds at the Manhattan skyline.

Mike's chest got tighter with each introduction. One of the women was Havers's New York counterpart, a special agent working white-collar crime. The other was from the International Operations Division. The two men were from the Counterterrorism Division.

"Coffee?" Havers asked. "A bagel or Danish, maybe?"

"I'm good."

"Okay, then let's get to it."

The group drifted to the table. Mike claimed a seat with his back to the windows. It was a small power play, just one of the many any negotiator worth his salt might employ, but it gave him the advantage of facing away from the bright sunlight.

He didn't derive much satisfaction from the maneuver. Not when he faced two counterterrorism agents. They left it to Havers to lay whatever cards they intended to share on the table.

"Here's the deal, Brennan. Your guy Montoya set off all kinds of alarms with his probe into that blocked account yesterday. We had to decide fast what to do about it. Especially when Montoya said you were on your way to New York. So we ran both of you through our computers. Every wrinkle, every wart."

"Find anything interesting?"

"Montoya is an open book. You read more like a tabloid."

"That so?"

"We know about the knife fight with the Portuguese cook when you were a ten-dollar-a-day deckhand," Havers commented. "We know about the navy medal you were awarded after diving into the Sea of Japan to save a crewmate who'd been swept overboard. We know you bought a rust bucket after you got out of the service and parlayed it into a multinational corporation. We know about your friends, your family, the divorce."

"What's your point?"

"My point is we wouldn't be talking to you today unless we knew we could trust you."

"Right now I can't say I feel the same. Cut to the chase. What's this all about?"

Havers angled his bull-like neck a few degrees to the right and nodded to one of the counterterrorism agents. Sandy haired and squinty eyed behind his wire-rim glasses, the other agent took the lead.

"What this is about is a guy named Thomas Danville and his five-thousand-dollar-a-week habit, which he feeds by skimming from his clients."

Mike felt his insides go tight but kept his voice even. "And?"

"And how this guy Danville buys his drugs from an international consortium. One that just happens to be headed by a terrorist organization whose stated goal is to wipe Israel—and its evil ally, the United States—off the face of the earth. You've heard of Hezbollah?"

Mike didn't alter his expression, didn't blink, but they'd just confirmed his worst-case scenario. Zia had gotten caught up in something a whole lot deeper and uglier than fraud.

"Yes, I've heard of Hezbollah."

"Then you might also have heard it has a substantial connection to the Mexican cartel Los Zetas. Two years ago we got an indictment in absentia against one of the middlemen acting on behalf of Hezbollah, a Lebanese drug lord by the name of Ayman Joumaa. Bastard conspired to smuggle more than 9,000 tons of cocaine into the US. In the process, he laundered over $250 million for the cartels.

"Look," he continued. "We don't give a shit about Danville. He's small change. Wouldn't even constitute a blip on our radar except for this drug connection. Nor would we be talking to you this morning if you hadn't started nosing around one of Danville's blind accounts. We need you to back off, Brennan. Now. Today."

Havers picked up the ball again. "We've been tracking Danville ever since one of his employees tipped us to his extracurricular activities. Problem is, he fired that employee yesterday."

Mike's eyes narrowed. "So you're worried Danville could be spooked."

"He could be," Havers conceded. "Though that's not all bad. Spooked guys make mistakes. Sometimes they run. Sometimes they turn to their big, bad pals for something to calm their jittery nerves."

"And sometimes," Mike said coldly, "they take innocent people down with them."

"Exactly. That's why we need you to back off. We've got taps on Danville's home, office and cell phones. We'll know if and when he makes a wrong move. Let us handle him, Brennan. Don't get in the middle of it."

"You're welcome to him. Like you, I don't give a shit about Danville. I do, however, care about—"

"Your fiancée. Yeah, we know."

Havers pursed his lips, as if debating whether to continue. The act didn't fool Mike for a moment. He sensed what was coming. Still, it hit hard.

"Danville and Dr. St. Sebastian enjoyed a three-hour lunch yesterday. According to one source, they got real close. Some might say cuddly."

Mike's reply came fast and flat. "For someone who wants my cooperation, you just went in exactly the wrong direction. This meeting is over."

He shoved back from the table and strode for the door. Havers had to scramble to catch up with him.

"Hold on, Brennan!"

He reached for Mike's arm. A low, savage warning halted his hand in midair.

"You really don't want to do that."

"Okay." He dropped his arm. "Look, I obviously pushed the wrong button there. I'm sorry."

Mike didn't bother to respond, just made for the elevator.

"Brennan! Wait. I have to escort you out."

He tried again to apologize but the elevator arrived too quickly. All he could do was follow Mike inside and ride down in silence. When they hit the lobby, though, he reached into his suit pocket.

"Here's my card," he said as they approached the security checkpoint. "Call me if there's anything else you want to talk about."

Mike came within a breath of telling him where he could shove the stiff, sharp-edged cardboard. He swallowed the urge, stuck the card in his wallet and tossed his visitor's pass on the security desk.

He used the rest of the morning to work the fury out of his system. A brutal workout in the hotel's exercise center helped. A long session in the steam room sweated out the rest. Showered and under control, he called Rafe with an update. His brother-in-law listened without interruption. At the end his only comment was a succinct and very graphic curse.

"Yeah," Mike drawled. "My sentiments exactly."

"How much of this are you going to tell Zia?"

"All of it."

"The FBI okay with that?"

"I didn't ask."

"I guess you probably didn't need to. They have to know you're not going to let her get in any deeper with this bastard Danville."

Let, Mike acknowledged wryly after he'd hung up, was the wrong verb. If he'd learned nothing else from living with three sisters and a moody ex-wife, it was to be extremely careful with that particular verb.

He shoved his hands in his pockets and wandered across the sitting room of his twentieth-floor suite. The wall-to-wall window offered an unimpeded view of One World Trade Center and, farther out, the Statue of Liberty. Mike let his gaze drift from one to the other, thinking of the jihadist pumping drugs into the United States, determined to destroy it one way or another. Thinking, too, of the thousands of little people caught in his poisonous web.

Like Danville.

And this employee Danville had reportedly fired.

And Zia.

Now him.

He'd charged right in, suspecting there was more to that blind account than mismanagement or misdirection of funds, and firing up like an Aegis missile when Havers and company confirmed it.

The more he thought about that visceral reaction, the more it bothered him. He didn't want to admit it sprang from that crack about Zia and Danville getting cuddly. He couldn't get around the implanted image, though. Not after Zia's wariness when Mike had told her he knew about the long lunch. Which, he remembered grimly, had come right on the heels of her saying she needed to talk to him. Maybe she already knew about Danville skimming his client's funds. Or maybe...

Christ! He had to stop chasing his tail like this. He'd

wait for Zia, talk it out with her, lay what he knew on the line and get it behind them both.

So he was more than ready when she called a little past three o'clock. "I'm just getting ready to leave the hospital. Are we still on for pizza and a movie?"

"I am if you are."

"Good. I skipped lunch so I'm starved. There's a John's Pizzeria right around the corner from the W. I'll call ahead and have a large regular crust waiting for pick up, all hot and gooey. What do you want on it?"

"Everything but anchovies or anything that resembles fruit."

"Got it. See you in forty-five minutes or so. In the meantime, you could check out the movies. I'm in the mood for something light and silly."

"Light and silly it is. See you soon."

Smiling in anticipation, Zia hit the off button and grabbed her coat.

"Pizza and a movie, huh?"

She glanced up to find Jordan Elliott smirking across the top of her computer terminal. The microbiologist's eyes reflected both mischief and envy.

"Sounded more like a little afternoon delight to me."

"What happens at the W, stays at the W."

"Oh, sure! Rub it in. You know very well the closest I've come to sex in the past month is watching bacteria multiply in a petri dish."

"I also know," Zia shot back, "there's a certain radiologist who's offered to fix that problem. Several times."

"Ugh. I'd rather cozy up to the bacteria. Hang loose a sec. I need to go over to the Infectious Diseases center. I'll walk out with you."

They exited the school of medicine and took the sidewalk that cut diagonally across Mount Sinai's sprawling campus. Spring was still weeks away, although the afternoon sun offered a hint of warmer temperatures and a sudden burst of greenery.

Zia was just about to peel off and make for the subway when her phone buzzed again. It was a text message from Tom Danville.

"It's Danville," she told Jordan, skimming the message. "He needs to talk to me ASAP about Elizabeth."

The two women exchanged quick glances. The Wharton School of Business grad's firing had shocked them both. Maybe now they'd discover what was behind it. When Zia called Danville, however, he didn't want to talk over the phone.

"It's an extremely sensitive issue. I need to discuss it with you in private."

"I don't have time now, Tom. I'm on my way to an appointment downtown."

"It'll just take a few minutes. You really need to know the mess Elizabeth's landed us both in."

She hesitated, chewing on her lower lip. "Where are you now?"

"At the office."

"All right. I'm just leaving the hospital. I'll swing by there on my way downtown."

Mike expected Zia by four. At four-thirty he hit the speed-dial number for her cell phone. When the call went to voice mail, he tried her office.

Her associate picked up and responded with a throaty chuckle when he identified himself. "Hi, Mike. Don't tell me you and Zia have already, uh, finished your pizza."

"We might have, if she'd showed up with it."

"She's not there? Wait. Scratch that. Of course she's not, or you wouldn't be calling."

"So she's not still at the hospital?"

"She left a couple of hours ago. I walked out with her, in fact."

"Did she take the subway?"

"That was the plan, but she got a call from Tom Danville. He said he needed to talk to her privately, right away, so she told him she'd swing by his office on the way downtown."

"I'll call you back."

"Wait! What's—"

He stabbed the end button and did a Google search for Danville and Associates. His jaw was tight and the cords in his neck as taut as hawsers. He knew what he would hear even before Danville's secretary confirmed that her boss had left the office several hours ago.

"Was Dr. St. Sebastian with him?"

"No," she replied in some surprise. "I'm looking at Tom's schedule now. He didn't have an appointment with her. Shall I—"

Mike slammed the phone down to search his wallet for Special Agent Havers's card. The FBI agent answered on the third ring.

"Havers."

"This is Brennan. Where are you?"

"On my way to the airport, getting ready to head back to DC. Why?"

"My fiancée was supposed to meet me at my hotel an hour ago. She hasn't showed."

"Have you—"

"She was on her way," Mike cut in savagely. "An associate walked out with her. The same associate just informed me that Zia got an urgent call from Danville. He needed to talk to her. Privately. At his office. But he left, and she never showed."

The pregnant silence that followed torqued his jaws so tight he could feel his teeth grinding.

"Listen to me, Havers. She's not having an affair with Danville. Nor is she in any way involved in his schemes."

When the agent still didn't reply, Mike pulled out every ace in the deck.

"My next call is to Dr. St. Sebastian's brother. He won't hesitate to tap his former sources at Interpol. Then I'm contacting Ambassador Harris at the UN. Then…"

"Hang up. Sit tight. Wait for me to call you back."

Mike's lips curled back in a snarl. "The hell I will. I'm going to hold on the line while you do the following. First, you contact your pals in the New York office. Second, you have them run a GPS trace on Danville's mobile phone. Third, you tell me where the bastard is."

"We warned you this morning to stay out of this, Brennan. We'll handle it."

"Call your pals, Havers. Now!"

Twelve

Zia just had to wait him out.

She'd stopped kicking herself for agreeing to meet Danville at his office. Gotten past the surprise of finding him in the lobby and ushering her into the elevator, only to send it down to the parking garage instead of up to his office. She'd also worked through her shock when he'd pulled out a small, lethal-looking pistol and aimed it at her heart.

Once her stunned mind reengaged, she'd recognized the signs. The fever-bright eyes. The agitation. The desperation. She'd seen it in patients, read about it in hundreds of case studies. Danville was in the panic stage. It usually set in several hours after the user's last hit. He would feel himself coming down and go frantic with the need to make sure he could score another hit.

If he didn't have a supply on hand, he'd beg, borrow or steal for it. Patients had reported pawing through their own and their parents' houses for something, *anything*, to pawn or sell. Others had robbed convenience stores, fast-food restaurants, even busy mall stores. The withdrawal is so intense, the craving so frantic, that they work themselves into a frenzy of need.

Danville was there. Jerky. Desperate. Paranoid. As he

forced her to get behind the wheel of the flashy red Porsche parked in his assigned slot, he kept mumbling they would kill him.

"Who, Tom? Who's going to kill you?"

"Drive! Just drive!"

She did. Up Madison Avenue, across 106th, down 2nd Avenue, with the pistol jammed into her side the entire time. She'd tried to talk him down. Tried to calm and soothe and assure him she'd get him help, but he was still locked in that hard, panicky shell. Checking his watch constantly. Flinching at every sound, every distant siren or screech of tires. And phones. Zia's. His. The buzzing must have ricocheted around in his mind like a loose ball bearing.

She'd considered crashing the Porsche into a street sign or traffic light, but she couldn't take the chance the airbags would explode in Danville's face before he pulled the trigger. So she'd followed his instructions until her shoulders ached with tension and her mind screamed with the need to do something, anything, to end the situation.

"There! Turn in there!"

She had to brake to take the ticket from the automatic dispenser at the entrance to the underground garage. Two lanes over, a bored attendant sat in his booth with his back turned so he could service exiting vehicles. Zia willed him to turn around, begged him to send just one glance her way. When he remained facing the other direction, she calculated her chances of yanking the door open and throwing herself out. Not very good with Danville's pistol bruising her ribs.

"Go down to the bottom level," he rasped at her.

She followed the winding ramp down five increasingly less crowded levels. The last was almost deserted.

"Pull into that space. The one beside the pillar."

The concrete column was square and fat but not difficult to maneuver around with so many empty spaces. Zia barely had time to wonder why he'd chosen that particular slot before she realized the pillar screened them from the security camera mounted in the corner.

Danville had been here before. Used this same parking slot. The realization hit like a balled fist to her chest. Fighting for calm, she cut the engine and angled toward him. He twisted in his seat, too, planting his back against the door, pulling the gun back with him. The bruising pressure on her ribs eased, but the barrel was still terrifyingly close.

"What now, Tom?"

"We wait."

She let her hand drop to her thigh, clenching and unclenching her fist as though driven by nerves. Which she was! But if she could keep him talking, keep his eyes on her face, she might be able to inch her hand into her tote, finger her iPhone, tap 911. The bag was in the space between their seats, just behind the gearshift console. So damned close.

"What do we wait for?"

"Not what. Who." He shot another look at his expensive watch. "They'll come," he muttered, more to himself than her. "Now that I can pay, they'll call off the dogs and deliver."

His suppliers, she guessed as the knot in her chest pressed hard against her sternum. She flattened her palm, eased it over the outside of her thigh.

"You cannot do this." She spoke evenly, slowly, but she could hear the American accent she'd acquired over the past two and a half years slipping away. "You cannot kidnap me, make me drive to this place, and think to get away with it."

Anger and a smirking bravado leaped into his face. Not a good mix with the desperation.

"Shows what you know! I've been getting away with it for years. Five thousand from one client, ten K from another. Eighty, a hundred thousand a year funneled into a special account the auditors never got a whiff of until that bitch started sniffing around it."

"Are you...? Are you speaking of Elizabeth?"

"Yes, Elizabeth." His lips curled back in a sneer that didn't quite match the fear and paranoia behind it. "She sicced the FBI on me. My...my associates found out about it. I don't know how. But they took care of her and now I have to cut and run. Today. Tonight."

Zia's stomach heaved. She'd ascribed his frenetic mood and barely controlled panic to crack. Now she knew it was due to something much worse, much uglier.

"How do you mean, they 'took care of her'?"

"It doesn't matter. She doesn't matter. *That's* what matters."

His gaze dropped like a stone and locked on the hand she'd slipped closer to her bag. For a frozen instant Zia thought he'd detected her cautious moves. Then she realized he'd focused on her engagement ring.

"I can't go back to my place. The FBI is probably watching it. I don't dare use my laptop or phone or credit card to withdraw the cash I need to pay my associates. But I can use that." He made a short, choppy motion with the gun. "Take it off."

"This is all you want from me?" she asked incredulously. "The ring?"

"Take it off."

She played the fingers of her right hand over the pear-shaped diamond. The faceted stone sat high in its mount. The surface was smooth, the tip sharp against her nervous fingers.

"You can have it, Tom. It is only a stone. Then will you let me go?"

He wouldn't meet her eyes, wouldn't answer her question. She knew then he would feed her to the dogs as cold-bloodedly as he had Elizabeth.

He had not the courage to do it himself, Zia thought on a burst of contempt. The men he waited for. They came not just to bring him the cocaine he craved. They would dispose of yet another problem female for him.

She twisted the band, tugged it toward her knuckle, pretended to have trouble getting it over the joint. "It's too tight. I…I meant to have it sized but have not had time."

"You'd damned well better get it off," he snarled, "or my friends will do it the hard way."

"So they are now your friends?" She couldn't keep the disgust from her voice as she twisted the band again. "A moment ago they were merely associates."

"It's none of your business wh—"

He broke off, his head cocking. Above the jackhammering of her heart, Zia caught the rumble of an engine. A vehicle was descending from the level right above them. A large, heavy vehicle.

"About damned time," Danville muttered, glancing over his shoulder at the ramp.

This was her chance! Her only chance! She didn't stop to think. Didn't weigh the odds. Fired by fear and utter desperation, she flayed out her arm and knocked the gun barrel aside. The violent action triggered an equally violent response. Shots exploded inside the sports car. One. Two. With blinding flashes. Concussive waves of sound. The searing burn of nitrate and the nauseous stink of sulfur.

Even before the shock waves died, Zia whipped her arm back. Ears ringing, eyes streaming, she curled her fist and put every ounce of her strength into a blow aimed for Danville's face. The force of it sank the sharp tip of her diamond deep into his left eye.

His eyeball exploded almost as violently as the shots had. Vitreous solution spewed in a clear arc. Blood gushed as Zia wrenched her wrist down and ripped through the lower lid. Howling, Danville dropped the pistol and slapped both hands to his eye.

She scrabbled for the gun with her bloody hand, but it

had fallen behind her seat. Not daring to wait another second, she shoved her door open and lunged out onto the oil-stained concrete. Her ears screaming, her cheek burning, she took a dizzy second or two to reorient herself. God help her if she ran up the down ramp and met Danville's *associates* head-on.

The brief hesitation proved a fatal mistake. A huge black SUV with darkened windows careened off the ramp less than thirty yards away. Zia whirled, then felt a scream rise in her throat when she saw Danville had crawled out of his car. Using the roof of the Porsche, he dragged himself upright. One hand still covered his oozing eye. The other gripped the pistol he'd recovered from the floor of the car.

Then everything happened in a blur. The SUV streaked by. Zia jumped back, barely avoiding its fender. It fishtailed to a screeching halt, and she dodged for the concrete pillar. Before she reached it, the SUV's passenger door flew open and Mike launched himself at the Porsche.

Danville whirled to meet this new threat, but the eye injury threw off his aim. The bullet hit the pillar just inches from Zia's head. Vicious bits of concrete bit into her still-burning cheek as the two men went down on the far side of the Porsche.

When Zia raced around the rear of the car, Mike was slamming his fist into Danville's already bloody face. She couldn't hear a thing above the screaming in her ears, but she saw his nose flatten and more blood gush through the shattered cartilage. Then a big, bull-like man rushed up and kicked the pistol away.

"Brennan! Enough."

He caught Mike's arm and hauled him off the now-unconscious Danville. Chest heaving, Mike shoved to his feet and spun around.

"Zia! Jesus!"

She saw his lips move but heard only a muted echo of

his words. She clung to him, her heart pumping fear and re-lief in equal measures until he caught her arms and gently eased her away. An oozy mix of blood and vitreous fluid now splotched the front of his saddle-tan leather jacket.

"Are you hurt?" His gaze raked her, searching for in-juries. "Zia, tell me where you're hurt."

She saw his lips moving again, heard the words as a tinny echo this time and shook her head. "I'm okay. This…." She had to gasp for breath. "This is Danville's blood."

And some of her own, she realized as she fingered the bits of concrete embedded in her cheek. Her hand came away filthy with body fluids and gunpowder residue.

The hulking man next to Mike said something. He was huge, with a loud, rumbling voice that was completely drowned out by the squeal of tires as what looked like an entire fleet of black-and-white patrol cars screeched down the ramp and onto their level.

She grabbed Mike's lapels and shouted to make herself heard. "Danville was expecting his…his suppliers. Here. Any moment."

"Hell!"

The next thing she knew she was being bundled into the back of a squad car.

"Get her out of here," the big man barked at the uni-formed officer behind the wheel, then shouted to two oth-ers. "And get this bastard to a hospital. Then the rest of you disperse. Now! Tune to my frequency for additional instructions."

The ringing in Zia's ears had subsided enough for her to distinguish his roared commands. She also heard the one he threw at Mike.

"You go with the doc, Brennan. This is our operation."

"It was." His mouth grim, Mike scooped up Danville's

pistol. In one smooth move, he hit the release, popped out the magazine and snapped it back in. "It's mine now."

The squad car Zia had been thrust into sped past the openmouthed booth attendant and took up a position a block away. Then they waited.

The ringing in her ears had lessened in volume but now had a sharp, shrill pitch. Tinnitus, she diagnosed. Not a concern in and by itself, but the accompanying numbness and tingling could signal a possible perforation of the middle ear. She fisted her hands and tried to ignore the metallic pinging while she waited. It couldn't have been more than a half hour but it felt like five before the radio squawked.

"Operations terminated. Four men in custody. All other units will be back in service."

"It's over?" she asked the uniformed officer.

"Yes, ma'am."

"Please, take me back to the garage."

He put the car in Park at the entrance and Zia waited anxiously for Mike to emerge from the dark tunnel. The moment she spotted him, she hammered on the Plexiglas partition.

"Let me out!"

Light-headed with relief, she threw herself at Mike for the second time that afternoon. As before, he held her gently. Too gently. She ached for the feel of his arms around her, but he eased her away and frowned at her cuts and powder burns.

"We need to get you to the ER."

"I'm…I'm supposed to wait and give a statement."

"The authorities can come find you."

By the time they reached the hospital her tinnitus had subsided to a bearable level. Enough, anyway, that she could hear the ER physician's diagnosis when he confirmed her own.

"You've sustained sensorineural damage in both ears.

The numbness and tingling in your right ear indicate moderate to severe nerve irritation. The ringing in your left may be temporary, but you should consult an audiologist as soon as possible."

"I will."

He rolled his stool back, looking as tired at the end of his long shift as Zia had so often felt. "We need to clean the debris from your cheek and swab it. Then, I'm told, the FBI wants to talk to you. There's an agent waiting outside."

She nodded but turned a surprised face to Mike after the door to the exam room closed behind the ER physician. "Did he say FBI?"

"Yeah, he did."

"How did the FBI get involved?"

"It's a long story. I'll tell you later."

The big, burly man from the SUV identified himself as Special Agent Dan Havers. He spent a good forty minutes walking Zia through her ordeal, from Danville's call to his gut-wrenching admission in the garage.

"He said that?" Havers demanded. "He said his friends had 'taken care' of Elizabeth Hamilton-Hobbs?"

Sick at heart, she could only nod. The FBI agent gestured for her to go on. She related the rest of the conversation, the momentary distraction of the vehicle on the floor above, her frantic swipe at Danville's arm, the ring she'd stabbed into his eye.

"Jesus!"

Havers shot Mike a quick glance but he didn't see it. His face was set in savage lines and his gaze had dropped to the gore still staining Zia's left hand. She couldn't tell whether he was pleased the engagement ring had proved so lethal or shocked she'd used it as a weapon.

She got her answer when he reached for her hand and

eased the ring over her knuckle. Face grim, he tossed it into the plastic-lined trash can beside the gurney.

"Hey!" Havers grabbed a glove from the box mounted on the near cabinet and shoved his beefy fist into it. "That's evidence. We need to preserv—"

"Preserve whatever you want. Then you can toss the thing in the East River, for all I care. Come on, Zia. I'm taking you home."

After a brief stop at the front desk to sign the necessary paperwork, he hustled her into a cab. Her ears were still tinny and every street sound seemed magnified a hundred times over. Still, she tried to dissuade him from calling ahead to alert the duchess.

When he insisted, the call resulted in exactly the chain reaction Zia feared. Charlotte alerted Dominic and Natalie, who arrived at the Dakota mere moments after Zia and Mike. Gina and her husband had been en route to a black-tie charity event and showed at almost the same time, Jack in his tux and Gina dripping sapphires. The duchess had even called Sarah, who'd begged for an update as soon as Zia and Jack explained everything.

The concern, the questions, the straining to separate their voices from the high-pitched ringing in her ear proved too much for Zia. With a pleading look, she turned to Mike.

"I need to wash and change. You tell them what happened."

Her departure left a stark silence in the sitting room. Mike squared his shoulders and faced her family. They were arrayed in a semicircle, Dom and Jack standing, Gina on the sofa holding Natalie's hand, the duchess in a high-backed chair gripping the head of her cane. Even Maria had come in from the kitchen to hear the details. All wore almost identical expressions of shock and concern.

Mike debated briefly where to start, then jumped right

to the heart of the issue that concerned them most—Zia's abduction.

"I don't know if Zia told you that she was working with a consultant to secure and manage the funding for her grant."

"Yes," Dom said shortly. "We know about that."

"Turns out this consultant—Thomas Danville—was skimming from his clients' accounts to support a cocaine habit. Evidently Danville was obtaining his coke from thugs working for a drug cartel with direct links to a known terrorist organization."

"What cartel?"

"Los Zetas. Which supposedly has ties to—"

"Hezbollah," Dom supplied, his jaw working. "And through them to Iran."

Hissing, he spit out something in Hungarian that whipped the duchess's head around. She said nothing, however, as he continued in a low growl.

"The Iron Triangle of Terror. And Zia got caught in the middle of this?"

"One of Danville's associates—a woman by the name of Elizabeth Hobbs—evidently became suspicious and contacted the authorities. Danville's suppliers got wind of it somehow and…"

A muscle worked in the side of Mike's jaw. He had to force himself to continue.

"According to Danville, his pals took care of Hobbs. At that point he panicked. He knew the authorities had to be on to him, tapping his phones, tracking his finances. He planned to skip the country but needed cash. And, apparently, another fix."

The grim account didn't get any easier with telling. An iron band seemed to tighten around Mike's chest as he finished in short, terse bursts.

"Danville contacted Zia. Arranged to meet her around three this afternoon. He pulled a gun on her, then forced her to drive to an underground garage. He intended to parlay her engagement ring into cash and coke. She used it instead to put out the bastard's eye."

The silence this time ranged from stunned to incredulous to furious. Gina broke it by pounding a clenched fist on her thigh. "I wish she'd jammed it down his throat!"

"Zia's face," the duchess put in. "The blood on her clothes. She was injured?"

"Danville got off a couple of shots at close range. One hit a concrete pillar mere inches from Zia's face, and her ears are still ringing from the percussive impact. The doc at the ER diagnosed the ringing as tinnitus but wants her to schedule an appointment with an audiologist for a more thorough check."

The family looked from one to another, still stunned, still processing the incredible information.

"Why didn't you call me?" Dom wanted to know. "Or Jack?"

"There wasn't time."

"The hell there wasn't. You just told us my sister went missing in midafternoon. You had hours to get hold of us. Unless…" Dom's eyes narrowed. "What *aren't* you telling us, Brennan?"

The razor-edged question brought Jack Harris out of his chair. Frowning, he stood shoulder to shoulder with his wife's cousin. "Cut the bull, Brennan. What do you know that we don't?"

Tension raced like a tsunami through the room. The force of it stiffened the duchess in her high-backed chair and caused her to rap out an imperious command.

"Sit down!"

She enforced the order with a vigorous thump of her cane. The solid whack pivoted the men around. Three bristling males who'd stormed or stolen their way into her heart. Jack so tall and tawny haired and sophisticated.

Dominic, her great-nephew, the grand duke, so dark and
dangerous looking. And Michael, with his wide shoulders
braced for battle and his green eyes refusing to yield so
much as an inch.

Charlotte couldn't have asked for a more impressive
set of genes to infuse the St. Sebastian family line. She
wouldn't admit that to them, of course, any more than she
would permit them to behave with such a lamentable lack
of manners in her presence.

"I must ask you not to ruffle your feathers and scratch
the dirt like fighting cocks in my sitting room. Sit down.
Now, if you please."

They obeyed. Slowly. Reluctantly. Charlotte tipped her
chin and waited until they were seated to pin Mike with
a cool stare.

"I, too, would like an explanation of why it took so long
for Zia's family to be apprised of the danger she faced from
this…this Danville person. Why didn't she tell us?"

"She didn't know the full extent of it until he abducted
her this afternoon."

"But you knew?" The duchess's snowy brows arched.
"You must have, to have enlisted the FBI's aid so quickly."

"An agent contacted GSI yesterday," Mike admitted, his
jaw working. "I met with them this morning."

"A fenébe is!" Dominic shoved to his feet again, his
eyes blazing. "You knew about Danville, and yet you let
Zia walk into his trap?"

"I didn't let—"

"What was she?" His fists balled. "Bait? A lure to bring
the bastard crawling out of the woodwork?"

"No."

Mike understood the man's fury. The same anger boiled
in his gut. He should've told Zia about the call from the
FBI last night. Failing that, he should've insisted she accompany him to Havers's office this morning. Instead, he'd

kept his damned mouth shut and she'd ended up fighting for her life. He'd never forgive or forget that monumental error in judgment.

Neither would Zia's brother. St. Sebastian moved on Mike, ignoring the duchess's gasp and his wife's quick word of warning.

"The FBI needed her, didn't they? To help nail their terrorist. *You* needed her, to recover your quarter million."

The charge was absurd. St. Sebastian knew that as well as everyone else in the room. Yet Mike didn't argue. Just waited for the punch *he* would have thrown if it had been one of his sisters in that dim, cavernous garage.

St. Sebastian ached to deliver it. Mike saw the primal urge in the man's bunched shoulders, read it in the flared nostrils. Then Dominic's dark eyes shifted to the right.

Mike followed the look and saw Zia standing in the arched entrance to the sitting room. She'd scrubbed her hands, combed back her hair and changed into sweats. Confusion and disbelief chased across her face.

"Did I hear right? The FBI contacted you *yesterday*? And you didn't tell me?"

Thirteen

Mike had only himself to blame for Zia's close brush with death. He couldn't escape that burden and didn't try. It sat like a stone on his chest as he related the sequence of events that had led him to the FBI.

First, Rafe's discovery of the overpayment of indirects. Then their suspicion funds were being diverted to a blind account. Mike's abrupt decision to fly to New York to discuss the discrepancy with Zia. Rafe's call relating the grim news that his probe had resulted in a call from the FBI. The request for Mike to meet with the agent this morning in New York.

His audience listened in stony silence. Zia, the duchess, Dom and his wife, Gina and her husband. The St. Sebastians had closed ranks, protecting their own, shutting him out. Mike's family would have done the same.

"I could have told you about it last night," he said to Zia. "I started to. Then…"

"Then?"

The single word was edged with ice.

"Then I played the odds," Mike admitted with brutal honesty as she entered the room. "I figured they had to know your background. I figured they'd also know yours," he said, meeting Dominic's stare head-on. "Europe's newest royal. Cultural Attaché to the UN. Former undercover agent. You think the Bureau didn't consider the possibility Interpol might come crashing down on them?"

His gaze shifted, pinned Jack Harris.

"Then there's you, Ambassador. Doesn't take a genius to grasp the political fallout if word leaked that the FBI was asking questions about your wife's cousin. And you, Duchess. You've become a celebrity. Again," he amended as her chin tilted.

"What has my aunt's status or that of anyone in my family got to do with your decision to talk to the FBI and not me?" Zia asked coldly.

"I thought they would talk to me more openly without all the heavy guns your family could bring to bear. The plan was to scope out the extent of the threat before I told you about it."

"*Would* you have told me if Danville hadn't abducted me and forced your hand?"

"Yes! Hell, yes!"

"How do I know that?" The frost didn't leave her voice, thick now with her native accent. "How do I know you do not think to protect me always? How do I know you won't shield me from everything that is dangerous or cruel or merely unpleasant?"

He opened his mouth, snapped it shut again. He wanted to assure her that he was modern enough, mature enough, to respect her as both an adult and a professional. Yet he couldn't deny the instincts imprinted in his DNA. Or was it RNA?

Hell, who cared? All Mike knew was that he was driven by the same need to shield his mate as every other living creature. He'd be lying if he denied it, so he pulled in a breath and spoke straight from his heart.

"I love you, Zia. I respect your drive and can't even begin

to appreciate your intelligence. But I'll always, *always*, try to protect you from harm."

That was met with dead silence. Mike thought he detected a glimmer of understanding in Jack's eyes, maybe even Dom's. The duchess looked cautiously noncommittal. But Zia had heard enough.

"I can't speak more about this now." She lifted trembling fingers to her bruised and cement-pitted cheek. "My face hurts and I still hear tinny cymbals in my ear. I'll call you, yes?"

When she turned away, Mike stretched out a hand. "Zia…"

"I'll call you!"

She whirled and left the room. To Mike's surprise, Dom rose and crossed slowly to where he stood. His dark eyes, so like his sister's, held marginally less hostility than they had before.

"I understand why you did what you did. I don't like the results, but I understand."

Mike snorted. "Can't say I'm real happy with the results, either."

"I know my sister. She won't be pushed or prodded. Give her time. Wait for her to call."

"And if she doesn't?"

"Then I would advise you to go back to Texas and forget her."

Yeah, Mike thought as he gathered his stained leather jacket and made for the door. Like that was going to happen.

Zia emerged from her bedroom into the stillness of the night, enveloped in the familiar comfort of her sweats and fuzzy slippers. An *un*familiar and unrelenting sense of loss sat like a stone on her chest as she negotiated the darkened apartment and shuffled into the kitchen. She flipped on the lights and filled the teakettle. While she waited for the water to heat, she rested both palms on the counter and stared blindly at the backsplash.

Her parents' death had shattered her. If not for Dom, she might still be mired in grief. He'd been her anchor then, and again during those long days after she'd nearly died herself. He'd buried his pain to help her work through hers. Brought her slowly, inevitably back to an appreciation of the joys life had to offer.

Yet Zia sensed—she *knew*—she couldn't turn to her brother to ease this hurt. He wouldn't understand how deep it cut. He couldn't. Although Dom would never admit it, he was every bit as possessive and territorial as any of their sword-wielding ancestors. Luckily he'd married a woman with the smarts and humor to tame those atavistic tendencies.

But Zia didn't want to "tame" her chosen mate. She wanted an equal. Was sure she'd found one. The realization Mike regarded her as someone to be coddled and protected blasted crater-sized holes in that erroneous assumption.

"Are you making tea?"

Lost in her thoughts, Zia hadn't heard the duchess's cane tracking toward the kitchen or the gentle swish of the swinging door. Her great-aunt stood on the threshold. She was wrapped in the fleecy blue robe Sarah had given her for Christmas and leaned heavily on her cane.

"I'm so sorry. Did I wake you?"

"Unfortunately not," Charlotte replied drily. "Sleep becomes extraneous when one reaches my age. May I join you?"

"Of course. The water's about to boil. Shall I make a pot of decaffeinated Spiced Chai?"

"Yes, please."

With the ease of long familiarity, Zia measured the fragrant tea into the infuser in Charlotte's favorite Wedgwood pot and added boiling water. While the tea steeped and released the tantalizing scent of ginger and cloves and cardamom, she filled a tray with two delicate china cups and saucers, a matching sugar and creamer, napkins, spoons and fresh lemon wedges.

She carried the tray to where the duchess waited in the breakfast room just off the kitchen. During the day, the room's ivy-sprigged wallpaper, green seat cushions and tall windows seemed to reflect Central Park at its joyous summer best. Even this late on a cold March night, the room served as a cheerful beacon in the gloom.

"There's something so soothing, so civilized about tea," Charlotte mused as she stirred milk into her cup. "Especially after such a brutal day."

Zia nodded and opted for lemon instead of milk.

"Are your ears still ringing?"

"Not as badly as before."

"And your face? Your lovely face?"

"The cuts will heal."

"Yes, they will." Carefully, the duchess replaced her spoon on the saucer. "Most hurts do, eventually."

"And some go deeper than others." Zia looked up from the dark swirl in her cup. "I'm not a child. Although Dom still tries to play the big brother, I declared my independence some years ago. I respect his concern for my welfare but I don't need him to protect me. I don't need any man to protect me. I thought Mike understood that."

"Forgive me, Anastazia, but that's twaddle."

"Excuse me?"

"Twaddle," the duchess repeated. "You're a physician. You know the male of the species better than most women. Their instincts, their idiosyncrasies. One of which is the belief that they're supposed to beat their chests and protect their females from all poachers."

The duchess's choice of words hit home. Mike had used the same word to describe Tom Danville after their first meeting. The noun ruffled Zia's feminist feathers almost as much now as it had then.

"Of course I know men are driven by primal urges. So are women. That doesn't mean we can't control them." She frowned, surprised by the direction the conversation had taken. "I thought you of all people would understand how I feel. You're the bravest, most courageous woman I know. You would never let someone wrap you in cotton wool and shield you from the realities of life."

"Oh, but you're wrong! You can't imagine how many times I wished for that cotton wool. For someone to block at least a little of the ugliness. And," she added with a sigh, "share the beauty."

"So what are you suggesting? That I should let Mike decide what to block and how much to share?"

"You must *both* decide. That's what marriage entails. Learning to respect each other's wants and needs and boundaries. It doesn't happen overnight."

"It certainly didn't happen today."

"Oh, Anastazia." The duchess stretched out a hand and folded it over Zia's. "I believe Michael only intended to… how did he phrase it? Scope out the threat. I also believe he planned to tell you as soon as he'd done that. Don't you?"

"I… Yes."

"And, my dear, I think you're forgetting one rather salient fact." She gave Zia's hand a brisk pat. "You're hardly a weak, helpless female. You didn't sit around and wait to be rescued. You incapacitated your attacker and escaped."

Those terrifying moments in the garage replayed in Zia's mind. Each graphic sequence, every desperate move. Including the heart-stopping seconds when Mike lunged across the Porsche.

"That's not entirely true," she said slowly. "I did incapacitate Danville and managed to get out of the car, but he still had his gun. Mike wrestled it away from him before he pounded the bastard into the pavement."

"He did that? Good for him!"

"He didn't tell you?"

"No."

Zia's surprise must have shown on her face.

"I suspect," Charlotte said drily, "he was more prepared to accept the blame for what happened than any credit." She let that sink in for a moment, then grasped her cane. "It's late and you've had a horrific day. You should get some rest."

"I will, I promise. As soon as I finish my tea."

"All right. Sleep well, dearest."

When the quiet thump of her cane faded, the apartment settled into silence. Zia cradled her cup in both hands and breathed in the last whiff of ginger and cloves from her cooling tea. The final moments in the garage kept playing and replaying in her mind.

"Dammit!"

Cutting off the mental video, she pushed away from the table.

The call dragged Mike from a restless doze. He'd hit the rack an hour ago and spent most of that time with his hands behind his head, staring up at the ceiling. After what seemed like hours, he'd finally drifted off.

When his cell phone buzzed he fumbled it off the nightstand. The number marching across the incoming display had him swinging his legs over the side of the bed and jerking upright.

"Zia? All you all right?"

"No. We have to talk."

"Now?"

"Yes, now. What's your room number?"

"My...?" He shook away his grogginess. "You don't need to come all the way downtown. I'll come there."

"Too late. I'm in the lobby. What's your room number?"

"Twelve-twenty."

"Got it. Now tell security to keycard the elevator for me."

After Mike gave his okay, Zia came back on the phone with a crisp, "I'm on my way up."

He pulled on his jeans, his thoughts grim. She'd told him to wait for her call. It had come a hell of a lot sooner than he'd anticipated. Too soon, his gut told him. She was still angry, still hurt. And very possibly suffering a delayed re-action to the traumatic events of the afternoon. He'd have to be careful, measure every word, or he'd screw this up worse than he already had.

He shagged a hand through his hair and made a quick trip to the bathroom. He barely had time to splash water on his face before she rapped on the door to his suite. He flicked the dead bolt, prepared for a kick to the gut when he saw her cut-and-bruised cheek. He *wasn't* prepared for the red-and-white cardboard carton she balanced on the palm of her hand.

"No anchovies or anything resembling fruit," she announced as she sailed past him with the carton held high. "I hope you have wine or beer in your minibar."

He stammered for a moment but finally managed, "I'm pretty sure there's both."

"Then I'll take wine. Red, not white."

She plopped the carton onto the counter that separated the living area from a small kitchenette and flicked on the overhead lights. The canned spots illuminated both the cuts and the determination in her face.

Mike was damned if he could interpret her confusing signals. Pizza and that lethal "we need to talk." Wine and utter resolve. Still wary, he uncorked a red and filled two wineglasses. She accepted hers with a cool word of thanks.

Ah, hell! He'd never been one for sailing at dead slow speeds. Might as well get the water roiling. Raising his glass, he tipped it toward hers.

"What should we drink to?"

She thought that over long enough to have him sweating.

"To us," she finally answered, "with certain caveats."

He brought his glass down. Slowly. Carefully. "I think I'd better hear what those caveats are before we drink to them."

"Smart man." She deposited her wine on the counter beside the pizza box and folded her arms. "Okay, here's the deal. I love you. You love me. But, as you no doubt learned from your previous marriage, love isn't always enough."

She had that right. Although Mike now wondered if he'd ever really loved Jill. Whatever he'd felt for her had certainly come nowhere close to this driving need to keep Zia in his life.

"So what do you propose?"

"First of all, no more scoping out situations on your own. No more independent threat assessments. We need to talk things out. Everything! The big issues, the little annoyances. Our families, our dreams, our fears."

"You want to talk all that out tonight?"

He was half teasing, half scared she meant it. Thankfully, his question elicited a muffled laugh.

"I supposed we can stretch out the discussion period."

The reluctant laugh told Mike he hadn't totally blown it. He moved closer, relief washing through him. "Stretch it out for how long?"

"Ten years?"

"Not long enough."

"Thirty?"

"Still too short." He caged her against the counter and felt himself falling into those dark, exotic eyes. "I'm thinking forty or fifty."

"Hmm," she murmured, sliding her arms around his neck, "that sounds about right."

A raw, gaping hole had ripped open when he'd almost lost her—literally and figuratively. She filled that emptiness now. The feel of her, the taste of her, was like coming home.

Sighing, she rested her forehead against his chin. "I was so terrified this afternoon."

"Who wouldn't be in that situation?"

"I wasn't scared for me! Well, yes, for me but for you, too. My heart stopped when you threw yourself at Danville."

"I was just the cleanup crew. You did the hard work."

She shuddered, and Mike wished savagely that he could have another ten minutes alone with Danville.

"You know," he said, to take her mind off the horror of the afternoon, "there's something we need to discuss that can't wait ten or twenty years."

She tipped her head back. "What's that?"

"When and where we're getting married. I vote for city hall, this weekend."

"This weekend!"

"As soon as we can get the license and blood tests done," he confirmed. "Your friends at the hospital lab ought to be able to help us out there."

"But city hall…"

"Or St. Patrick's or the chapel at your hospital or the top of the Empire Building. You pick the place, I'll take care of the arrangements."

"You can't! I mean, we can't. Gina would have a fit."

"What's she got to do with it?"

"Gina's an event coordinator! She does only a few select events now that she has the twins, but she's still one of the best in the business."

"Fine. Ask Gina to arrange it. For this weekend."

She leaned back in his arms. "This is your idea of talking things out?"

"Well…" He tried to sound apologetic but couldn't pull it off. "Pretty much."

"I'll get together with my cousin," she said, holding his eye sternly, "and come up with a list of options for us to discuss. You. Me. Together."

Mike had no problem with that. He'd achieved his primary objective of getting her mind off the horror of this afternoon. Even more important, he had her thinking when, not if.

"Fine. Now let's talk about whether we're going to eat pizza or go to bed. You. Me. Together."

She melted into a smile. "Bed. Now. End of discussion."

Fourteen

Gina pulled out all the stops and coordinated two separate events.

The first was a May wedding that took place in Galveston a week after Zia completed her residency. They did it Texas style, with Mike's male relatives and friends in either formal Western wear or Spanish-style suits. The women wore lacy dresses in a rainbow of colors. Even the New York contingent got in the spirit of things, with the duchess looking especially regal in a tall ivory comb and exquisite white lace mantilla purchased for the occasion.

The Camino Del Rey resort erected a portable pavilion that stretched from the dunes almost down to the water's edge. Filmy bows with sprays of bluebonnets decorated the white chairs. Long, fluttering white ribbons tied additional clusters of bluebonnets to the pavilion's tall poles.

Mike's three brothers stood shoulder to shoulder with his brothers-in-law. His three sisters joined Gina and Sarah and Natalie on the other side of the dais. Little Amalia and Charlotte made prim, dainty flower girls, in direct contrast to the fidgeting, reluctant ring bearers, Davy and his brother, Kevin.

Mike's parents and *abuelita* sat with the duchess in the

front row of seats. Aunts, uncles, cousins, friends and acquaintances of both families filled the rest. But Mike had
eyes for no one but his bride when she walked down the
aisle on the arm of her brother.

She'd caught her ebony hair back and crowned it with a
garland of white roses, but the sea breeze played with the
ends. The glossy black tendrils danced around her face as
she and Dom matched their steps to Franz Liszt's "Liebe-
straum No. 3." Or maybe it was one of his nineteen rhap-
sodies. Mike figured he'd learn which was which in the
next ten or twenty or thirty years.

Then he took Zia's hand in his and refused to let his
gaze linger on the spot where she'd worn the diamond.
She hadn't wanted another engagement ring. Just the wide
gold band he'd had inscribed with what had become their
personal mantra. With a smile in his heart, he recited the
words to her now.

"You. Me. Together. Forever."

Gina coordinated a second event that took place less
than a week later, just before the start of Zia and Mike's
extended honeymoon trip to all her favorite haunts in Hungary and Austria. This event took place on a rocky prom-
ontory guarding a high Alpine pass between those two
countries, with the ruins of Karlenburgh Castle forming a
dramatic backdrop.

The number of people in attendance was considerably
smaller than the Galveston event. Just Zia and Mike. Dom
and Natalie. Sarah and Gina and their husbands. The twins,
bundled against the cool mountain air. And the Grand
Duchess of Karlenburgh.

It was the first time she'd returned to her homeland since
she'd fled it more than sixty years ago. She stood alone,
both hands resting on the head of her cane, the ruins behind her, the sun-dappled valley far below. She didn't seem

to notice the wind that molded the skirt of her pale green traveling suit to her hips and fluttered the scarf she wore around her neck in a fashionable double loop. Her gaze was fixed on the distant horizon. Her family could only guess what she saw in those lacy clouds.

"She must be remembering the first time she came here as a bride," Gina murmured, maintaining a firm grip on Amalia while Jack kept Charlotte corralled. "She was so young. Barely eighteen. And so much in love."

"Maybe she's thinking of the balls she and our grandfather held here," Sarah said softly. "How I wish we had a photo or portrait of her in sables and the St. Sebastian diamonds."

"Or she may be remembering Christmases past," Dom put in quietly. "The last time Natalie and I were here, we talked to an old goatherd. He still remembered the tree-lighting ceremony in the magnificent great hall. Everyone from the surrounding villages was invited."

Zia folded her hand into her husband's, aching for the woman she'd come to love so fiercely. Zia and Mike were just beginning their life together. So much of Charlotte's was past and shrouded with sadness.

The duchess's eyes drifted shut for a few moments. Her right hand lifted a few inches, moving in a small, almost imperceptible wave. Then she regripped the ebony head of her cane and squared her shoulders. When she turned to face her family, her chin was high and her eyes clear.

"Thank you for talking me into returning to Karlenburgh. I shall always remember this moment and I'm more grateful than you can ever imagine that I was able to share it with all of you. Now for pity's sake, let's go down to the village. I could use a good, stiff *pálinka*."

Epilogue

What an amazing summer this has been. My darling Sarah has given birth to the most exquisite baby girl. Dev is beyond thrilled and sends me detailed and rather exhaustive reports on her gurgles, her burps, her every hiccup. Gina and Jack stood as her godparents, then just weeks later Natalie and Dom announced that they, too, would be adding to the ever-increasing St. Sebastian clan.

Anastazia and Michael are so very busy with his business and her work. Her research, I'm quite pleased to note, has expanded to such an extent that she travels extensively to other universities and hospitals around the country—most often to University General Hospital in Houston, I must note.

She and Michael talked about starting a family. I took great care not to insert myself into that discussion, of course. But it couldn't have been more than three weeks later that Maria called, frantic with the news that she'd found a toddler wandering down her street wearing only a soiled diaper. Anastazia rushed over immediately to examine the child. It's a crack baby, as addicted to drugs as its mother must have been when she